ORDER 86
BY
ALEX PAXTON

This is a work of fiction. Names, characters, places, and incidents either are the product of the author's imagination or are used fictitiously, and any resemblance to actual persons, living or dead, events, or locales is entirely coincidental.

CHAPTER 1

Theirs was a love that was forbidden, at least that was what company policy dictated. They had been working very closely for almost a year and nature had taken its course. What had started out as an occasional break time meal, grew into drinks after work, and eventually a dinner date. They were discreet, since neither wanted to lose their job, but they knew that eventually their feelings would get the better of them.

One late night, not so long ago, they had a break through on their current project and, in a moment of elation, they kissed. At the moment it had felt like the natural thing to do but they had become conscious of their surroundings and being observed by surveillance cameras. They broke their kiss and the embrace, but what the cameras could not see was the look in their eyes that they would recapture in better surroundings.

Later that night, after celebrating the break through with colleagues, they did just that. They decided to go to her place, since it was closest, and there was a 24 hour drug store on the way. Their passion finally subsided, in the early hours of the morning, and he left to go home before giving in to exhaustion.

The following day was a struggle to keep up appearances, since all they wanted to do was jump each others bones like a couple of horny teenagers. The two eventually refocused that energy on their work and made progress, in fact; they were now three days ahead of schedule. The affair went on for the next couple of months. Driven work ethic, with laser-like precision during the day, with passionate stolen moments at night.

They ended up completing their project three weeks ahead of schedule. The president of the company rewarded the department with a paid four day weekend.

To avoid raising suspicion, the couple agreed to see each other only three nights a week. They decided to break that rule and use the four days for a real celebration. He made reservations at a luxury hotel, using an assumed name, since it already felt a little naughty. The master plan was to turn off their phones, hang a "Do Not Disturb" sign on the door, and order room service all weekend. Company policy and the rest of the world be damned.

They had not been in the room for even an hour, when things started to heat up. She smiled, grabbed a small bag, went into the bathroom, and closed the door.

He quickly undressed and placed a box of condoms on the night stand before sliding under the covers. He checked his watch.

"What's taking so long?", he asked the closed door.

She heard the question and smiled, checking her hair in the mirror.

"I'm almost ready." she said loud enough for him to hear.

"Are you sure about this?" she said in a low voice to the reflection.

The earpiece made an electronic click before a voice said, ("Intel is confirmed. Proceed with operation.")

She took a deep breath and let it out slowly as she nodded to herself in the mirror. She turned and opened the door to reveal a white bathrobe that covered her from just below the knees to where she had it pulled closed to her neck. He had a quizzical look as he eyed the robe. She untied the belt slowly and

3

let the robe fall open exposing a matching set of very small, very lacy bra and panties. Sliding it off her shoulders, she let the robe fall to the floor.

"Well?" she asked.

"I approve." he responded.

She moved to the bed and straddled his waist while running her hands over his chest and shoulders.

("Immediate termination authorized")

She moved her hands to his neck as the sound of broken glass was heard before she fell forward. At first he thought it was still part of the seduction but when she did not move he thought something more serious was happening.

He rolled her onto the bed next to him, and as he pulled his hand out from under her he noticed blood. He scanned the room in confusion. What had caused this? What could he use to stop the bleeding? Was there a doctor in the hotel or should he call 911? Where did that hole in the window come from? That was the last thing to go through his head before the bullet.

The couple had been careful, in

case anybody happened to observe them, but someone had been observing, and the fact that they were a couple had made the job that much easier.

A man was on the opposite rooftop disassembling his long range rifle and folding up the tarp he had used for camouflage. Within two minutes, he was making his way down the stairs, with what appeared to be an attache case in his hand. Just another business man, burning a little midnight oil, now on his way home.

CHAPTER 2

His name was Frank Emerson and he had worked hard all of his life. Work hard, play hard; that was his motto. It paid off in school, and it paid off at his job. He had multiple awards for his work in the computer field, and he had recently made the cover of Science Magazine. He enjoyed being outdoors when time allowed. Trail biking, camping, paint balling, and sky diving were some of his favorite past times.

He had not had time for anything outside of the computer lab as of late. He was hard at work in the final stages of Project Wildfire. Three other departments answered to him; he was the maestro who was to put all of the pieces together.

Wildfire was technically a worm, but when he had to explain it to the people running the project he referred to it as a virus; which was easier than trying to explain the difference. The "virus'" objective was to infiltrate technology systems and replicate until it completely took over the host system.

Frank removed the SD chip from its secured container, and placed it in a holder that he plugged into an isolated laptop. The screen began to fill with binary ones and zeroes, which soon changed to all zeroes, before the laptop shut down becoming an overpriced paper weight.

Frank felt proud, like a new father but, at the same time, the horror of knowing that he had orchestrated a monster. It was not a question of in the wrong hands it is evil, but in the right hands it is beneficial to mankind. It was simply, that if this thing ever got out, it would throw the world into a tailspin of finality. Frank knew what he needed to do, but first, he had to get his creation as far away from his project heads as possible.

Frank pulled a coin out of his left pants pocket and a metal ring out of his right. He used the ring to open the false coin, before setting it on the desk. After putting the chip into the coin half, he married the two pieces back together. Having marked an X on it, he blew on the coin to dry the ink before putting it back in his pocket. He then retrieved a pen and paper from his desk drawer and started to write a note.

CHAPTER 3

Jen was startled to consciousness by the digital blaring of her alarm clock two feet away from her head. She ran through a mental checklist as she turned it off, I'm clothed, I'm alone, I'm at home. She had had the same morning routine since college where she had majored in theater. Now it felt like all she had was the alarm clock, the checklist, and a monthly statement telling her how much she still owed for the experience. She rubbed the sleep out of her eyes and went to the kitchen to make coffee.

On the way, she noticed the light blinking on her answering machine. One day she would join the twenty-first century and get a cell phone and stop being the butt of her friends jokes when they could not get in touch with her instantly, but today was not that day. One day, she would get a dream role that would make her a star, but today...might be that day. As the message played, she heard Murray, her agent, reminding her again about the days events.

"Jen, honey, don't forget you have that audition for "The Magician" today. I never heard back about those magic tricks I sent you. I hope you've been practicing. Anyway, break a leg, hon."

"Oh, shit." Jen muttered to herself. She had been practicing for the last few days but it was not going as well as she would have liked. She walked into her living room and picked up a fifty-cent piece next to a book on sleight of hand. She started manipulating the coin over her fingers as she thumbed through the book in search of the section on making it disappear. She managed to flip the coin from her thumb to her little finger, but dropped it on the return trip.

CHAPTER 4

Frank finished the letter, folded it, and placed it into an envelope along with the ring used to open the coin. Still on schedule according to a nearby clock. He would leave the envelope to go out with the morning mail, and be on his way before anybody missed him. Yes sir, he thought, as long as I can avoid any stumbling blocks, this should run like clockwork. He had just pocketed the coin when Anne walked in. Frank moved around the desk to head her off; he still needed to tidy up.

"Hi, Frank."

"Anne, good morning, what can I do for you?"

"You don't happen to have any coffee, do you? We ran out yesterday and Amanda's supposed to bring some, but she's not here yet."

"No, I haven't brewed any yet, just had to take care of a couple of things before I am back out the door."

"You work too hard."

"Deadlines, what can I say?" He checked his watch. "Could you do me a favor?"

"Anything for you, Frank."

He pulled the envelope out of his lab coat pocket.

"I need this delivered by nine this morning and I'm already late for jury duty. Could you take care of it for me?"

He placed the envelope into her waiting hand.

"I didn't know you had jury duty."

"I almost didn't either. Just found out last week; I should probably check my mailbox more often. I thought I told you about it. If I'm lucky they won't need me. Can I rely on you to get that messengered by nine?"

"You can count on me. Why'd you wait until the last minute?"

Frank tried to sound a little embarrassed, "I forgot! Okay, look, just forget it. I'll take care of it myself."

Frank tried to retrieve the envelope but Anne took a step back.

"I said I'd take care of it and it'll be done, just go do your civic duty, and you owe me dinner."

Frank stepped forward and gave her a peck on the cheek.

"You got it. You're the best."

They walked out of the lab, and

closed the door behind them.

"Thanks again." Frank said before turning to leave.

"You're welcome, and good luck."

Anne turned to go back to her office. She glanced at the envelope in her hand, "Julius Rosenberg" was written in block letters. The name sounded familiar but she could not quite place it. He must have been one of the independent contractors they dealt with, there were too many to keep track of.

She sat at her desk, picked up the phone and dialed the operator. All the while, just under her breath, in a conga rhythmed sing-songy voice repeated,

"me and Frank and din-ner, me and Frank and din-"

"Good morning, how can I help you?"

"Can you put me through to Speedy-Bike Delivery, please?"

As Anne waited for the connection, she absent mindedly drew a small heart on the envelope, continuing the sing-song.

"Hi, this is Anne Banner over here at Lassiter International. How quickly can I get someone to take a delivery?"

She heard the tapping of keys.

"Probably going to be a good couple of hours, we're pretty slammed this early in the day."

"You don't have anyone available sooner?" Anne asked, almost whining. She heard herself and responded to her own question.

"You know what, never mind, I'll take care of it myself. Thanks."

"Okay, sorry about that, have a good day." the voice on the other end of the phone said.

"Yeah, thanks, you too."

She hung up the phone, frustrated with the circumstance and herself, for almost turning into one of those women that she loathed. She checked he schedule, and saw that she had some time. Since Frank's project was complete, her mornings were free. She could find the address, deliver the envelope, and be back with an hour to spare.

Looking at the envelope, she noticed the heart she absentmindedly doodled. She picked up the pen and scratched it out, hoping that the recipient would just remove the contents and dispose of the envelope. She grabbed her purse from the bottom drawer, and started for the parking garage.

CHAPTER 5

Jen had moved on from coin tricks to illusions. She was consulting the book while attempting to pull a scarf out of a false thumb. The feed would get tangled and end up launching the prosthetic half way across the room. Jen growled at herself in frustration.

CHAPTER 6

As Anne made her way to the elevator, she found Stan, head of security, making a routine inspection of the laboratory floors.

"Good morning Stan. What's new?"

"Hello Anne. Same ol', same ol'." He checked his watch and noticed the early hour. "Are you just coming in or finally going home?" he asked, nodding at her purse.

"Oh, I, uh, just have to run a quick errand. I forgot to pick up some things on the way in." she replied, hoping the lie did not sound as obvious as it did in her head.

"The morning rush should be thinning out by now. Should be pretty easy going," Stan replied.

"Right, well, the sooner I get going, the sooner I will get back." She wanted to be on her way but just then an idea came to her. "Say, is there anything you or the top floor can do to help Frank get out of jury duty?"

"What do you mean?"

"He was called in. Didn't you know?"

"I wasn't aware he had jury

duty."

"I've known for weeks. I just hope he can get out of it before we-" she was suddenly aware of who she was talking to, it would not do to confess to a company policy violation before it even got that far, "before we, uh, fall behind on a project."

"Yeah, that could be unfortunate. To answer your question, there might have been something the company could have done to help, under the circumstances, but if he's getting called up now, there's nothing we can do."

"I was afraid you were going to say that. Oh well, never hurts to ask, right?"

And with that, she turned and walked to the elevators. Stan watched her get on and when the door closed he fast-walked to Franks office.

CHAPTER 7

Jen was again consulting her book of magic tricks, using one hand as the other was handcuffed to an exposed steam pipe. She rolled the shackled wrist as the diagram depicted, but without success.

She happened to notice the clock, 'damn', she thought, 'I have to get ready for work.' Dropping the book, she attempted to free herself using both hands; again, without success. Searching for the key, she noticed it on the table...across the room.

"Shit."

CHAPTER 8

Stan looked over Franks office. Nothing seemed out of the ordinary, with the exception of the empty microchip holder on the desk. He checked the secure container and noticed the empty slot. Immediately, he picked up the phone and dialed an office extension, and barked out,

"I need a secure line to Mister Lassiter, now!"

"Authorization code?"

"Authorization Security Alpha one five nine."

He waited for the transfer, and heard his boss' voice answer.

"Mister Lassiter, sir. This line is secure. Wildfire is missing. I found the empty chip holder and Emerson left for the day."

"Are you certain?"

"He told a co-worker he had jury duty, but there was nothing on his calendar this morning."

"You know our clients have a special arrangement to avoid these kinds of distractions."

"That was my thought as well, sir. Orders?"

After a pause, "Implement Order Eighty-six."

"Sir, isn't that a bit extreme?"

"If Wildfire is initiated, there will be no way to contain it. Get that chip at all costs. If we can capture the lab tech as well, fine. If not, so be it. This is not the time to take chances!"

"Yes sir."

Stan hung up the office extension, retrieved his cell phone from his jacket pocket, and speed dialed his second in command. The man answered after one ring, he only heard his boss' voice.

"Priority Alpha. Apprehend Frank Emerson."

In the elevator, Frank studied his reflection in the steel door, took a deep breath, and told himself to act naturally; he would be out of the building before anybody was the wiser. He reached up and straightened his tie; the picture of confidence.

CHAPTER 9

Jen was still handcuffed to the pipe. Her attempts to reach the key, even laying down and stretching her foot across the room, came up short. She had to find something to extend her range, but what? Her phone was out of reach and there was nothing else.

"You have to think outside the box", she kept telling herself.

Then, she noticed the standing lamp in the corner. She realized the answer was on her. Jen took her pajama bottoms off, grabbed one leg with her free hand, gave her arm a quick shake, and the pants unfurled as she threw her arm forward, flicking her wrist at the last second. Bingo! She hit the lamp...but not with the desired effect.

'Okay', she thought, 'this isn't going to be as easy as it looks in the movies.' She tried again. When she saw the pajama leg wrap once around the lamp she tugged quickly, hoping to knock it off balance. It teetered but then righted itself. She repeated the action and as it rocked back toward her, the lamp toppled.

'Almost there', she thought. Sitting down and stretching her leg out, she hooked the lamp with her foot. She was pulling it slowly towards her when it stopped. Adjusting to see what had snagged her progress, she noticed the cord, pulled to its full length, still in the wall.

"Well, shit."

CHAPTER 10

Frank was going through exiting security procedures; placing his keys, loose change, and cell phone in a tray, and waiting. Hardly anybody left at that hour of the morning, so the emphasis was on the line of people coming in to work. His mouth suddenly went dry as he heard a voice behind him call out his name.

"Mister Emerson."

It was Eddie, the chief of lobby security. Frank turned to face the voice.

"Didn't mean to startle you. I just wanted to let you know that my wife loved that baklava recipe you gave me. She asked me to give you this, it's her famous chicken soup. She doesn't give this out to just anyone."

Eddie placed the recipe in the tray with Franks other belongings. Franks heart rate was returning to normal as he walked through the metal detector. Eddie met him with the tray.

"I'm glad to hear it." Frank said. "I'd stay and chat but I'm in kind of a rush at the moment."

Eddie gave him a smile.

"No worries, Mister Emerson. I'm looking forward to the next one."

"I'll get right on that." Frank said as he started redistributing his belongings.

"Take care." Eddie said as Frank turned to leave.

"Yeah, you too." replied Frank.

"Stop that man!"

"Don't let him leave!"

Two security agents in black suits exited the stairwell and ran across the lobby toward Frank. The crowd around the elevators were rubbernecking with interest after the pair.

Frank noticed a man on his cell phone in the incoming line. He cut in behind him and tapped the man on the shoulder.

"I think they're looking for you." Frank said.

"Wait a second, hon." the man said into his phone. Turning toward Frank, he asked, "excuse me?"

Frank motioned at the approaching agents.

"Let me call you back when I get in." the man said into his phone.

He went to put the phone into his inside coat pocket when Frank gave him a bump forward with his shoulder while yelling,

"Oh my God, he's got a gun! Look out!"

Just then one of the security agents went through the metal detector, setting it off and adding to the chaos. The line turned into a mob as people were either heading for the exits or trying to figure out which direction to run.

Frank made it out the door just in front of the crowd, but the first security agent got caught in the melee.

Eddie had dialed only 9-1-, when the second security agent depressed the disconnect button on the receiver.

"Put that phone down." was all he said to Eddie.

"The procedure is to call it in." Eddie responded, annoyed.

"This is an internal matter, possible industrial espionage. We've got it."

Eddie reluctantly replaced the handset. The second security agent fought his way outside to assist his partner.

"Damn," Eddie muttered, "what have you gotten yourself into, Frank?"

CHAPTER 11

Anne left the elevator and got into her car. She removed the envelope from her purse, set it on the seat, and the purse on the floor. She put the address into her GPS device before starting the car and pulling out of the parking garage.

Frank had hidden himself in some shrubbery at the corner of the building. He could see the security agent looking for him and he also noticed a second agent join in the hunt. While the two agents headed off in opposite directions, Frank proceeded in a third and tried to blend with pedestrian traffic. He stopped to buy a hot dog as he saw the traffic thinning out. Using the food stand for cover, he took his time searching for both agents as well as anybody else who might have joined the chase.

"Want a dog, mister?" asked the vendor as he noticed Frank lingering in his area.

"Sure" Frank replied absently, his eyes still scanned the area. The vendor went through his pitch.

"I got franks, Polishes,

Italians and burgers if you want, with or without cheese."

"I don't care. Your cheapest." Frank responded, just trying not to arouse suspicion.

"Okay, big spender here. Waddaya want on it? I got mustard, ketchup, mayo, relish, onions, sauerkraut...", the vendor trailed off, anticipating a response. Frank, realizing there was nobody around, suddenly joined the conversation.

"Mustard. Just mustard."

The vendor prepared the dog and presented it to Frank.

"Okay, that'll be three fifty."

Frank reached in his trouser pocket and pulled out a five dollar bill and handed it to the vendor. After exchanging the bill in his apron pocket and making change from a holder on his belt, the vendor turned back to Frank.

"And your change." The vendor fumbled and dropped the coins. Frank bent down just as one of the security agents walked past. Frank saw the agent and stayed crouched a little longer. The vendor tried to put the bill into the cash box. A gust of wind combined with the vendors fumbling fingers sent the bill riding on the wind like a leaf. The vendor attempted to grab the

bill, but was unsuccessful. He saw
it floating towards a small group
of people.

"Hey, somebody grab that bill!"
he yelled to them.

"Dammit, the boss is gonna kill
me if I come up short again." he
muttered to himself.

The vendor's effort to reclaim
his prize had everybody's attention,
including Franks pursuers. Frank saw
his chance, stood up and walked away
at a natural pace tossing the
uneaten hot dog into the nearest
trash receptacle.

CHAPTER 12

Using the lamp, Jen had managed to hook the leg of the table and was able to drag it to her. The vibration of the moving table, unfortunately, caused the small key to slide off.

"Damn" was all Jen could say in her moment of frustration, "damn, damn, damn, damn!"

CHAPTER 13

Rounding the corner and running half way down an alley, one of the pursuers realized he had lost his man. Frank had crouched in the shadows of the dumpsters. He was planning to let the security agent pass and then double back in the opposite direction. Unfortunately, the agent had decided to break off pursuit and go back to regroup. Frank had to change his plan. He knew he had to be quick and when the moment came he cold cocked the agent square in the jaw.

The agent went down, his gun skittered across the ground. Frank followed up with a kick to the head and the man was unconscious. Frank ran over and picked up the gun, aimed it at the unconscious man, but hesitated to kill him. He was just a man doing a job, like himself. He could just take the gun and keep running.

Before Frank reached a decision to pull the trigger or not, there was a searing pain in his hand as two shots rang out in succession. The first one grazed his hand, causing him to drop the gun and recoil in pain as he felt the second fly through the space he had just occupied.

Frank looked up the alley and saw a black SUV with the shooter leaning out of the passenger window. The SUV only had a foot and a half of clearance on either side in the narrow alley so Frank turned and ran for the far end as fast as he could. He had rounded the corner as the SUV pulled up to the unconscious agent who was beginning to stir.

CHAPTER 14

Jen was still trying to maneuver the unwieldy floor lamp to snag the small keys, but her hand was cramping with the effort; she eventually had to drop the lamp. She shook out her hand and reached over to massage her cuffed wrist which was sore from being pulled to its full extent. As she did, the cuff opened.

"Are you kidding me?" was all she could say. Noticing the time, she sprinted for the bathroom, pulling her sleep shirt off and angrily throwing it across the room.

CHAPTER 15

Frank had made it two blocks where he found cover behind another trash bin. He ripped the lining from his jacket and managed to bind his wounded hand. He was considering his next move when he saw one of his pursuers run by. Luckily, he was not seen and the man kept moving down the sidewalk. Frank was about to make a break for the next alleyway when he heard an SUV round the corner and slow down. The vehicle proceeded down the side street just below ten miles per hour. They were looking for him to double back.

Frank got low and out of sight as the SUV passed. He took a couple of deep breaths and, running in a crouch, he moved in behind the vehicle. Keeping low, he stayed with the SUV until it was just past the alleyway he was headed toward. While still in a crouch, he ran into the alley and stopped long enough to make sure that the vehicle was not coming back. Seeing that it did not follow, he stood up and continued down the alley.

CHAPTER 16

Jen had finished drying her hair and was putting on her work shirt as she grabbed her purse and headed out the door.

***

Frank spotted someone close to the end of the alley. His first thought was to seek cover but, he noticed that the man did not see him. In fact, he did not seem to move at all. Upon further inspection, Frank realized that it was a homeless person just looking for a place to sleep. He approached cautiously.

"Hey, man. Are you awake?" Frank inquired of the unmoving form. There was a small stirring and then a response.

"Wha? Wassup?"

"Hi, what'll you take for your coat?"

"You got any spare change?" said the homeless man, more out of conditioned response than opening a negotiation.

Frank countered with, "I'll give you twenty bucks for your coat. Deal?"

The other man pondered this for a second and replied, "Sure. Hey, you got a down payment on a cheeseburger?"

Desperate but approaching frustration, Frank said, "Look, here's forty", he produced two bills and held them up for the man to see. "And you never saw me, got it?"

The other man considered Frank's offer and then responded, "That's a nice belt, mister."

Frank had to admire the man for being able to make the most of a desperate situation but, at the same time, he was getting annoyed by the shakedown. He took off and handed the man his belt, along with the two twenty dollar bills. "It's yours. Do we have a deal?"

"Sure" said the other man as he started to remove his coat.

"And you never saw me?"

"Saw who?" the man said as he exchanged coats with Frank.

"You got it, pal. See ya."

Frank put on his new coat and considered going back the way he came, figuring the coast might be clear. He thought better of it and decided to go to the small cafe across the lot.

Anne's GPS told her she had reached her destination, but she double checked the address, since the slightly run down apartment building did not look like anything their regular contractors would have lived in. Deciding she had the right place, she picked up the envelope, exited and locked her car, and walked through the main door of the complex.

CHAPTER 17

Patty was a morning person; she had been for as long as she could remember. She liked being part of the world as it came to life to start a new day. That was why she liked working the early shift at the diner. She could wake up, start her day, make breakfast for her and her son, see him off to the bus and still have time to make it to work. They were never exceptionally busy for the breakfast rush but those that showed up were dedicated regulars.

Along with regular paying customers, there was also the constant stream of homeless that came through. Some of them would actually have enough for a cup of coffee or a bowl of soup, but then they would always stick around for an hour or longer. They were not as bad as those who would come in and just order water and think that qualified them as a customer. The worst were the ones who would come in and order a meal and then try to sneak out when they were finished.

Doug, the owner and cook, eventually just told the girls not to let anybody in that looked homeless. It was not worth the hassle.

As Frank entered the diner, he tripped over the threshold as he tried to close the door behind him. 'Great', Patty thought, 'another one, and an early morning drinker to boot'.

"Hey mister" Patty called to Frank as he closed the door. "No bums allowed."

Frank was caught a little off guard, but he reached into his pocket and flashed a money clip with folded bills.

"I can pay" Frank said with an I-come-in-peace tone to his voice, "do you have a phone here?"

Patty gave Frank a look that told him only his best behavior would be tolerated, as she pointed towards the back. "It's over there."

Frank nodded, thanked her, and walked over to make a call. He fumbled for his change, while keeping an eye on the front door.

* * *

Anne found the apartment and was about to knock, when the door suddenly opened. The man, who opened the door, did not invite her in, in fact he barely spoke. She could only see part of him through the open crack; the room behind him was dark.

"Are you Julius Rosenberg?" she asked of the man.

He only nodded. She handed over the envelope, he looked at the address, and noticed the scratched out heart doodle.

"Thank you" was all the man said.

Anne smiled uncomfortably and turned to leave. 'These independent programmers are a weird bunch', she thought.

CHAPTER 18

Time was of the essence.
Schedules had to be kept and there
were a lot of call to make. If done
properly, the person making the
calls stood to make a lot of money,
since this would ripple around the
world. The caller picked the first
number they remembered and, with a
voice modulator in place, proceeded
to make several calls.

It was night time in Moscow
when a phone rang in the office of
the SVR. The director had gone home
for the night, but there was always
somebody in the office; to answer
calls, take instructions from a
foreign office, or anything else
that should need attention in the
night while defending the secrets of
one of the worlds super powers.
Usually, it was just boring clerical
work.

"Da?" a man answered.

"Lassiter's marble is outside
the circle. If you want in the game,
the buy-in is triple the usual
price." a disguised voice had said,
and then hung up.

The man's English was rusty but
he understood enough to know that he
should call the director. The

director could listen to the recorded message and proceed from there.

Around the world, similar scenarios were playing. The mysterious voice had called all of the worlds intelligence services and repeated the same message, along with information on where and how to ante up if they wanted further information. As soon as all the bids were in, the caller would start round two. In the mean time there was much work to be done.

CHAPTER 19

Jen finally made it to work. Hoping to avoid getting a lecture from Doug, she went in through the front door, but Patty was waiting in ambush.

"It's about time you got here, girl. Where've you been?"

"A magical land of wonder and pain. Did I miss anything?" was Jen's response.

"Naw, just the usual. I don't know why Doug doesn't lock that back door. We got another weirdo." Patty jerked a thumb toward Frank who was leaving the phone booth and sitting at a table.

"Oh, I've seen worse. Remember the guy with–"

"The face!" they both said in unison. They shared a laugh as Jen tried to twist her face.

"Yeah, fine" Patty said, "you wait on him. Consider it penance for showing up late."

Jen stuck her tongue out at Patty, then went behind the counter to exchange her purse and jacket for an apron. She walked over to Frank's table, where he was glancing out the window.

"So, what'll you have?"

"Just coffee, thanks."

"Cream, sugar?"

"Lots of cream, honey."

Jen smirked at the joke. 'Set myself up for that one', she thought. She walked back to the counter to get his order.

Frank inventoried the contents of his newly acquired garment, and found a handful of change; apparently it was a slow day on the panhandling front. He put the coins back in the coat pocket and reached into his pants pocket for the fake coin. He flipped it through his fingers as he contemplated his next move. He set the fake on the table as Jen came back with his coffee and a bowl of creamers.

"Coffee and lots of cream, just like you asked."

"Thank you." Frank said distractedly as he noticed two of his pursuers moving down the street. He moved the bowl of creamers to cover the coin and added cream to his coffee as he noticed one of the security agents looking through the window. Frank leaned in a little to put Jen between himself and the man at the window.

Turning to Jen, he asked, "You come here often?"

"No, I just like to put on this outfit, walk into strange restaurants and serve customers. It's kind of my thing."

Frank smiled and replied, "Me too. We've got a lot in common."

"So how come you're sitting at the table instead of getting your own coffee?"

"It's my day off."

Jen chuckled as the security guard Frank ambushed walked through the front door. He looked around at the customers, his attitude an even match for his bruised face. Doug saw him and stepped out of the kitchen.

"Have a seat anywhere."

"I'm not eating, I'm just looking."

"Hey pal, this place is for customers only. You ain't paying, you ain't staying."

The security agent took another look around. He could see the handful of customers along with the two waitresses and some guy in a ratty looking coat drinking coffee.

"That's okay" the security agent said, "I'm not seeing what I'm looking for. It wouldn't hurt you to be a little more hospitable."

"You gotta pay me to be hospitable, buddy."

The security agent made a gun with his forefinger and thumb, smiled as he pointed at Doug, then turned and left the cafe.

Frank saw the man leave and breathed a sigh of relief. Knowing when to press his luck and when not to, he turned to Jen.

"Well, it was nice talking with you, but I've gotta run. Could I get the check, please?"

"You've barely touched your coffee."

"I know, and I wish I could stay, but I'm late for a previous engagement."

"Don't be a stranger, stranger. My name's Jen."

"I'm Frank. Say, would you mind taking a picture for my memoirs?"

Jen considered the request then said, "Sure, why the hell not?"

Frank held up his bandaged hand.

"Would you mind? It's a little difficult for me."

Frank handed her his cell phone; Jen leaned in and took a picture of the two of them. As she did this, Frank slipped the fake coin into her pocket.

"This'll make your girlfriends jealous."

"I don't have a girlfriend at the moment."

"Play your cards right and you never know what can happen."

From a look in Frank's eyes, Jen started to wonder if she'd gone too far.

"I'll get your check, now."

Jen turned back to the counter to get the check as Frank typed a text message, attaching the photo. 'Check out my waitress friend. She's a hottie. I need air conditioning. BTW: what do all treasure maps have in common? Tell you the answer when I see you.'

Frank was checking out the window again as Jen handed him the check. He looked at it and dug in his pockets for enough change plus a tip. He left the money on the table and waved to Jen. He then darted out the door in the opposite direction from the security agents and jumped into an idling cab.

Patty walked over to Jen and asked, "Did you just take a selfie with that guy?"

"Yeah."

"If he had a working cell phone, why did he want to use the pay phone in back?"

"I don't know. That is strange."

"You really shouldn't be taking selfies with strangers. You could end up on a porn site."

"Jesus, Patty, we weren't doing anything embarrassing. Really, what's the worst that could happen?"

CHAPTER 20

The cab driver, an older jovial fellow, looked at Frank through the rear view mirror.

"Where to, my friend?" he asked in a distinctive accent.

"Just drive for now. I'll tell you where in a little bit."

"As long as meter runs, you are boss." the driver said. He put the car in gear and headed down the street.

Two of Frank's pursuers noticed the cab and the one with the bruised face gestured for the SUV. As it pulled up, the man got in and indicated to follow the cab. The other men got into parked cars and followed. The man in the SUV picked up a radio mic and started talking.

CHAPTER 21

Stan's office almost seemed like two rooms. On one side, a desk, nice but not extravagant, with a chair that looked like the most comfortable piece of furniture on the whole floor. There were some monitors, mounted on the wall, that allowed him to see every camera in the building. There were also a couple of book cases, close to the desk, with technical manuals and other reference material. On the other side of the room, there was a small table with two chairs. Nothing fancy; just practical. That's where Anne was sitting. She felt like she had been called to the principals office.

Stan was sitting across from her, trying to be casual and put her at ease. He was not succeeding. His first instinct was to grab her out of her office, tie her to a chair and make her tell him all that she knew. He would have her talking inside of ten minutes. But this was not the good ol' days of working with banana-land dictators. He had to be patient, and use a little finesse.

"Thank you for coming." he said,

as if she were in a job interview. "This is just a formality." He was interrupted by his cell phone ringing. "Pardon me." he said, getting up from the table and moving across the room.

He pushed the button to answer the call.

"Yes sir?"

"I just received a disturbing call from our client."

Lassiter's voice sounded controlled, but Stan could hear anger and frustration bubbling just underneath.

"He seems to think that Wildfire has been compromised. Where would he get such an idea?"

"I don't know, sir."

"Find the leak and plug it. Permanently."

"Already on it, sir." Lassiter hung up, and Stan turned his attention back to Anne.

"So, Anne, how well do you know Frank Emerson?"

Anne, caught a little off guard, seemed a little shy and aloof as she said, "Well, you know, it wouldn't be right for a girl to kiss and tell."

Stan raised an eyebrow at the response. "Really?" was his verbal reply.

CHAPTER 22

Jen cleared the dishes, scooped the money into her apron pocket, and wiped the table down with a clean rag so it was ready for the next customer. She reached into her apron pocket for the money, to start tabbing out the register, when she felt something odd. She pulled out the coin Frank had slipped into her pocket and looked at it, unsure of where she had picked up a fifty cent piece. She figured it must have been part of the change that Frank left, and she just had not noticed it. She glanced at the table where he had been sitting; the pleasant memory made her smile.

Inside the cab, Frank kept looking behind for anybody tailing them. The cab was winding its way through the streets; so he figured any pursuit vehicle would stand out. Suddenly, he heard his cell phone indicating an incoming text message. He looked at the screen, the caller was listed as UNKNOWN. The message read: 'Girl too hot to handle? I'll hit that for you. P.S. Maps???'

'Dammit', Frank thought, 'nothing is going right today'. He

kept looking out the window, willing the cabbie to go faster.

CHAPTER 23

Having finished questioning Anne, Stan was now alone in his office. He was on the phone with his boss, who sounded like he had calmed down. Stan's progress report seemed to be helping.

"The tech arranged for a coworker, Anne Banner, to deliver a package."

"Was it the chip?"

"Unknown. It could be."

"How did he manage that? We were under lock down."

"Poor timing, sir. Banner left before the lock down was fully communicated."

"Where is the package now?"

"I have the address. I've dispatched a team. Emerson may have more than one accomplice within the building."

"Find out what you can. I want the chip at all costs. I want Emerson alive, if possible. Order Eighty-six is still in effect. Are we clear?"

"Crystal. I'm on it, sir."

"Good man."

Stan hung up after Lassiter had disconnected the line. He put the transcript of the Banner interrogation into a folder, placed it into a file drawer, and closed and locked the drawer. It contained a few files and some miscellaneous communication equipment, but it would not do to have the head of security lax in his protocols. He punched the intercom button and then two more digits. An assistant answered. Stan told him to send up the first guard from the lobby security detail.

CHAPTER 24

After a few turns down the city streets, Frank could see his destination up ahead.

"Pull over and drop me off here."

"You got it my friend."

The driver pulled to the curb. Frank got out looking around to see if he had been followed. Satisfied, he tossed a few bills through the passenger window that he had fished out of his pocket. The driver rapidly collected them.

"Are you wanting change my friend?"

"Keep it." was all Frank said before dashing across the street, dodging traffic. He ran up to the building and ducked inside.

The driver turned off his car and got out. He looked at the doorway where Frank had gone and just shook his head. He was surprised that his fare had managed to live so long. He walked over to a newspaper machine, deposited money and removed a paper. Leaning against the hood, he resigned himself to reading until the next fare.

CHAPTER 25

Upon confirming the money in an off shore account, the mystery voice informed all of the interested parties.

"Be warned. A free agent is playing for all the marbles. Lassiter has initiated Order Eighty-six to put the genie back in the bottle. Any outsider exposed to Wildfire will be liquidated. Tread carefully."

CHAPTER 26

Stan's next interview was with Eddie, the chief of lobby security, who worked the front door checkpoint. Eddie had been in the security business for several years and understood the importance of the L.I.E. contract to his employers, which was why he tried to be as forthcoming and reassuring in his answers. Stan wished the man would just get to the point.

"Eddie, did you and Frank trade recipes often?"

"Oh yeah. My wife is always looking to try something new and Frank always had really good tips on how to improve the food. You know, unusual spices and stuff. My wife would try it out, and then tell me things to pass on to Frank as well."

"And you did this often?"

"Oh yeah. Mister Emerson's a stand-up guy. Whatever you think he did, I know he's innocent. Take my word, I can read people. Ask anyone."

"I'm sure it will all be cleared up in due time. I do a little cooking myself. What kind of spices did Frank recommend?"

"Oh, you know, things like

turmeric and herbs de Provence. And
he always made sure the specific
proportions were precisely correct.
That's the key, you see. He really
knew his stuff."

"Tell me more."

CHAPTER 27

Frank was removing the homeless man's coat, when his cell phone rang. The caller I.D. told him it was Anne.

"Frank?"

"Now is not a good time to talk."

"They're looking for you. I told them about that package you gave me."

"What did you tell them?"

"Just that it was some paperwork for one of our contractors. That is what it was, right?"

"Dammit! Why couldn't you keep your mouth shut? Did you tell them the address?"

"Frank, what's going on?"

"DID YOU TELL THEM?!"

"Yes. Yes, I did. I'm so sorry."

There was a click as Frank hung up. He ran out of the building, barely closing the door behind him. He hailed a cab that was heading back downtown.

Frank and his new driver were discussing a destination as the cab pulled into an intersection, and was T-boned by a black SUV, coming down a side street.

The driver that brought him was

still leaning against the car
reading his paper when he heard   the
crash down the street.

CHAPTER 28

The mood in Stan's office seemed more relaxed and Eddie was glad for that. He still had a hard time believing that Frank Emerson, the same guy who always had time to stop and converse about the day and exchange recipes with his wife, could be capable of anything bad.

"Thanks, Eddie, you've been very helpful. I'm sure it's all been a misunderstanding. You can go now."

As Eddie got up to leave, he could not help commenting, "You bet it's a misunderstanding. Frank Emerson is a good guy."

Stan was interrupted by his cell phone ringing. "I'm sure he is. If you'll excuse me, I have to take this."

"No problem, sir. No problem at all." Eddie said as he left the room, breathing a sigh of relief as he closed the door.

Stan turned his attention to his phone call.

"Speak."

"We have him, sir." said the voice of one of the agents he sent out to retrieve Emerson.

"Have you recovered the chip?"

"Not yet, sir."

"Send him to Bess, she'll persuade him."

"There's a civilian, sir."

"No loose ends."

Stan hung up the phone and considered his next move.

CHAPTER 29

Jen stood at the cash register
exchanging her tips for larger
denominations, when she spotted the
coin with an "X" on it. She did not
remember picking it up; but after
thinking about it, she put it back
in her pocket. She checked her watch
before looking up to see Doug at the
grill.

"Hey Doug, I've gotta go to my
doctor's appointment."

Doug came out of the kitchen,
"What doctor's appointment? You
didn't say nothing about no doctor's
appointment."

"I told you about it two weeks
ago and reminded you again last
week."

"What's it for again?"

"Female problems. You don't want
me getting all PMS on you, do you?"

"You women and your female
problems. Get outta here. But I'm
gonna dock you a day's pay for
leaving me in a bind like this."

"No you won't."

"And why not?"

"Because it's illegal, because
it's not that busy, because I'm not
leaving you in a bind, and because

you love me and you know it." She flashed him a big smile.

"I need you back to help with the dinner rush, though. You'll be here?"

"I'll be here."

Jen reached up and gave his cheeks an affectionate pinch. Doug rolled his eyes and laughed.

"Go on, leave, before I decide to examine you myself."

"Jesus, Doug." Patty said as she heard the last part of the conversation. Doug went back into the kitchen; Jen grabbed her purse from under the counter. As she walked to the door, she turned to Patty.

"Do you think he bought it?"

"Honey, like I told you, mention 'female problems' to a man and he doesn't want to hear any more about it. Now you go to that audition and you get that part."

"Thanks, Patty, and thanks for covering for me. I owe you one."

Jen turned and walked out the door.

"Good luck to you, honey."

Doug walked out of the kitchen just in time to hear Patty's last comment. He looked at her questioningly.

"Good luck?"

"You know, with her female problems."

"I don't wanna know." Doug walked back into the kitchen, unsure of why he left. Patty smiled to herself and checked on her customers.

Jen left the diner, running through a mental checklist of everything she would need for the audition. She took no notice of the dark haired man sitting at one of the outside tables, casually drinking coffee. He noticed her though, and giving her a half block lead, he finished his coffee. He set the cup down and was standing up when he noticed somebody else, across the street, notice Jen.

The dark haired man at the diner, paused for a moment to see what action the stranger would take, and then scanned his surroundings to see if anybody else was going to start following the girl. Satisfied, he got up, and followed both the stranger and Jen.

Jen turned a corner, and bumped into a woman with her dog walking home from the grocery store. Her shopping bag upended and the contents spilled onto the sidewalk. Jen stopped to help, while the stranger nonchalantly window shopped. The dark haired man following both of them stopped to tie his shoe.

"I am so sorry, I guess I'm just in my own world today." Jen said as she bent down to gather the bags contents.

The dog stuck his nose in Jen's face, and was about to lick her cheek, when the woman pulled him back by the leash.

"Dudley, no!" she said. "Not everybody wants you in their personal space. Now, sit!" Dudley sat. "Sorry" the woman said, "he thinks everybody is a dog person."

"Oh, he's fine. That's a beautiful dog." Jen said, rising and handing the bag, now refilled, back to the woman.

"Thank you." the woman said, "where's a pretty girl like you off to in such a rush?"

"I have an audition and I don't want to be late."

"Wow, an audition. Did you hear that Dudley? We bumped into an up and coming celebrity. Is it for television? You're not going to be in one of those violent zombie programs, are you?"

"Ha! No, no zombies. It's a

movie. They're turning the old Bill
Bixby show, The Magician, into a
film. They"re gender swapping the
lead so I'm off to audition."

"I don't see many movies. I
prefer television. But, good luck
anyway."

"Thanks." Jen said as she
hurried home.

The woman and the dog walked
down the sidewalk. The dark haired
man finished tying his shoe.

"Good afternoon, young man."

"Afternoon, ma'am." was all the
dark haired man said as he proceeded
on his way.

Jen walked into her apartment,
pulled all the change out of her
pockets, and put it in a jar. She
hung on to the coin with the X,
pondering it for a moment.

"Just in case." she said,
dropping it on top of her monologue,
and headed to the bathroom to
freshen up.

Outside, the stranger, who
followed her home, was leaning
against an adjacent building, trying
to look natural. He walked to the
corner of the building, phone in
hand when, he felt a hand cover his
mouth and a sharp piercing pain in
his lower back. Everything faded to
darkness; he crumpled to the ground.

The dark haired man, who had followed Jen and the stranger, gathered his deceased burden and deposited him around the corner, next to the dumpster. With his hands in his pockets, he strolled, innocently, toward a shade tree and sat down at an angle, that half concealed him, while allowing him to watch the door of Jen's building.

CHAPTER 30

In a quiet unassuming suburban two story house, a woman chopped vegetables. Her immaculate kitchen had every modern convenience. It was where she spent most of her time, and did her best work. She softly hummed an old gospel tune as she prepared a stew. Adding the vegetables to a simmering pot, and efficiently cleaning the knife and cutting board, she set a stove timer for twenty minutes, smoothed her apron, and turned her attention, across the room, to the two men tied and gagged in chairs.

Frank Emerson, and his most recent cab driver, stared wide-eyed as the woman approached, a motherly smile on her face and a chopping knife in her relaxed hand. Frank tried not to portray his fear, as his mind raced to figure a way out. The cab driver was already trying to plead and bargain through the gag.

"Now children," the woman addressed them, "you've been very, very bad. You realize that, don't you?"

Frank and the cab driver looked at each other bewildered, and then back at the woman. The cab driver resumed his muffled pleading.

"I'm sorry, sweetie. Were you trying to say something?" She reached across and removed his gag.

"Lady, just let me go, please. I ain't got nothin' to do with whatever you got goin' here. Please just let me go. I won't say nothin', I swear. I'm just a cab driver, for Christ's sake!"

"Don't take the name of the Lord in vain, young man, that's blasphemous."

"I'm sorry. I'm so, so sorry. Please forgive me, ma'am."

"Now that's much better, young man. Don't you feel better?"

"I do. Yes, ma'am. I really do."

The motherly smile returned, as the woman continued.

"So, you're a cab driver? How nice. I'm guessing no one even thought to tip you. Would you like a tip?"

The cab driver's breathing had almost returned to normal as he said, "That's really not necessary, ma'am. Just let me go and we'll call it even, okay?"

"No sir, I'm going to give you a tip."

She leaned in close to whisper in his ear, "When you follow a recipe, always use half the amount of salt they tell you to. Now, that's a vey good cooking tip."

The cab driver was silent as the woman stood back up. He slumped forward as she raised her blood covered chopping knife and cleaned it with her apron.

"The poor boy wanted to be free, and now he is in the arms of Jesus."

She turned to face Frank.

"I'm so sorry, Mister Emerson." she said, moving closer to him. "I forgot to introduce myself. How impolite of me. Manners matter, don't you think? You can call me Bess." Raising her knife to inspect its cleanliness, she added, "So, Mister Emerson, what do you have to say for yourself?"

CHAPTER 31

Jen boarded the bus, paid the fare, and took her seat. She had just started reviewing her monologue, when a man sat down in front of her. He had an obnoxious pop song playing on his phone, at a loud volume. Her concentration broken, Jen tapped the man on the shoulder, attempting to get his attention. After three attempts, he turned to face her.

"Would you mind turning that down a little? I'm trying to concentrate."

"What's the matter, don't you like music?"

"Sure, just not when it's being played for people at the next stop, and I'm on my way to an audition."

"What-evs, lady." the man replied, and pulled out a set of ear buds.

Jen flashed him a smile; he turned back around with a sour expression. Five seconds later, he was moving his head to the beat.

Jen turned her attention back to her monologue, but became re-distracted when she noticed the ink on her thumb from rubbing her new lucky coin. She wiped most of it off, with the help of the seat and tried again to focus on her monologue. She never noticed the dark haired stranger at the back of the bus, watching her under the bill of his cap.

CHAPTER 32

Stan beckoned the security guard into the small windowless room.

"Come on in, and close the door."

The security guard did as he was told, and walked further into the room.

"Have a seat." Stan said, motioning to a plastic chair opposite a small table between them. Again, the security guard did as he was told.

"How well do you know Frank Emerson?"

"Uh, not well, sir. Just to say hello, really."

"Eddie tells me that he and Frank traded recipes a lot. Interesting, don't you think? Do you like Eddie? Think he's a good guy?"

The security guard was relaxing a little, seeing that he was not going to get chewed out for the morning's debacle concerning Emerson.

"Uh, yes, yes, sir."

"Did you ever think that maybe those recipe ingredients were some sort of code between the two of them?"

"No, sir. I mean, I never really gave it much thought. But it might have been." The security guard considered the possibility and continued. "I mean it definitely could have been some sort of code."

"Do you think Eddie might be a spy? The man is close to retirement. I don't think he has set much aside to live on. Is it possible that he and Frank were selling secrets?"

The security guard was more than happy to cooperate with anything that did not involve him getting fired, plus, Stan was making sense, his supervisor had been behaving oddly.

"WOW! Yeah, I never really thought about it, but that makes sense."

Stan leaned a little forward.

"Tell me your suspicions. Don't worry, you're not in trouble here. Let's start with those recipes."

CHAPTER 33

Jen took a deep breath and approached the receptionist desk.

"Hi, I'm Jennifer Rosewood. I've got an appointment."

The young woman sitting behind the desk smiled, and did her best to make her instruction sound like she was giving it for the first time.

"Sign in over there. Put your name, phone number, e-mail and agency. Then take a seat. They're running behind, so it'll be a while. There's coffee if you want it."

Jen turned around to see the crowd of people sitting, waiting to audition. With a heavy sigh, she filled out the paperwork and sat, greeting those around her with a smile. She didn't notice the stranger from the bus, who sat down in the row behind her.

CHAPTER 34

Stan stood in front of Mr. Lassiter's desk as Lassiter glanced over the transcripts of Stan's interviews. After a long moment he looked up and addressed the security head.

"Report."

"We searched the lab. Emerson definitely took the Wildfire virus. We've got him; but not the chip. Bess is questioning him now. She'll get results."

"That she will. What about Wildfire?"

"he claimed that he lost it. We discovered who accepted delivery of the package Emerson sent." Stan added with discomfort.

"Am I supposed to guess?" Lassiter snapped.

"He was using the name Julius Rosenberg." Stan said, as he placed a photo on Mr. Lassiter's desk.

Lassiter looked at the photo and sighed audibly.

"Him again. The bane of my existence. Oh, Samuel, Samuel, Samuel. Do you think he has the chip?"

"It's possible, but I don't

believe so, sir. If Samuel had the chip, Emerson would have just skipped town. We believe Emerson made a drop somewhere, most likely at the cafe."

"Who else did Emerson contact?"

"He spoke to an Anne Banner. I interrogated her and she insinuated that they had a personal relationship."

"Is she our songbird?"

"Doubtful. She's stupid, but not malicious. She sent the package without verifying the contents. I've made arrangements for her to be taken care of, along with the front desk guard. He's my top suspect right now."

Lassiter skimmed over the transcript of Eddie's interview.

"I think it's best if I handle him personally, for morale." Stan continued.

"Any other loose ends?"

"The diner, the gypsy cab driver, and Samuel. That's it."

"Handle it. Make it quick and painless for Samuel, but I want Emerson alive and able to talk. As its designer, he's our best hope of creating a controller for Wildfire."

"I understand, sir."

"No you don't. In its current

state, Wildfire could destroy us all. I can't stress this enough. We need the chip and we need what's in Emerson's head. Am I being repetitive?"

"Actually...yes, sir."

"Good, because it's that important for you to understand."

CHAPTER 35

Jen, feeling good about her audition, walked back into the reception area to collect her belongings. She passed a dark haired man reading the newspaper; and headed toward the door. He put down his paper, rose, and headed for the exit when his path was blocked by the receptionist.

"I believe it's your turn now."

"I've changed my mind, I'm not ready to audition."

"Oh, don't let your nerves get to you. You never know, this might be the one. You won't know until you try."

"Really, I'm just not up for it."

The receptionist let him pass as she consulted her clipboard for the next auditioner. Before he made it out the door, his path s again blocked. This time it was by a man in a brightly colored shirt and top hat, holding a fan of playing cards in his hand.

"Pick a card" he said while waving his free hand at the fan with the flourish of a game show hostess, "any card."

The dark haired man picked a

card and showed it to the magician.

"Ace of Spades. You win."

The man flicked the card at the magician, and ran out the door, in search of Jen. He spotted her, half way down the block, getting onto a bus. He ran for the bus, but it pulled away right as he reached the corner.

When Jen finally got home, she rushed into her apartment and turned off the alarm. Any good feelings she had about the audition, were cast aside with her clothes when she realized how late she was running.

CHAPTER 36

Deep inside the headquarters of the National Security Agency, in a private office, was a phone conversation nobody wanted overheard.

"We have retrieved the tech who developed Wildfire and we expect to have the chip in our possession shortly." said the voice on the other end of the receiver as the caller sat at his desk, listening. He was not happy about what he heard.

"I don't want to hear you're going to have it, I want to hear that it's already in your possession. Both our asses are on the line here."

"We've tracked it to a cafe downtown. I've dispatched a recovery team."

"What about the mole? What progress have you made?"

"My head of security is on it. He has several leads and has made arrangements to eliminate all suspects."

"So you think this is contained?"

"Order Eighty-six has been highly effective so far."

"It never should have reached the point where Order Eighty-six was necessary. I hold you personally responsible. If this gets out, I'll skewer your head on a pike myself!"

"Well, Director, that is a colorful image. Need I remind you that I have collected heads more powerful than yours?"

"Just get it done!"

The NSA Director hung up on Lassiter. A moment later, he picked up the phone and dialed his secretary. It was a short moment before she answered.

"Put me through to agents Brown and Greene."

CHAPTER 37

Jen was tying on her apron as she entered the cafe, her mind occupied with a hundred different ways to apologize for her tardiness. Her eyes were still adjusting from the bright sunlight, when she first noticed that there was not the usual noise level associated with that time of day. When her eyes finally adjusted to the fluorescent interior, she stopped in her tracks. She saw Patty and Doug lying dead on the floor next to one of the counter customers. Another customer was slumped over in a booth to her right, and somebody, was that Frank from this morning?, was sitting on the floor with his hands bound in front of him. Somebody in a dark suit was sitting at the counter, to her left, next to him. Another dark suited individual was behind the counter messing with a box of something in the doorway of the kitchen.

"Hurry up. We need to blow this place before anyone else shows up." The dark suit at the counter was talking to the one in the doorway.

"Omigod!" Jen exclaimed, still standing where she had stopped.

The man in the doorway looked up, saw Jen, and then looked at his partner.

"Get her!"

Before the man on the stool could react, Jen turned and ran for the door. Her way was suddenly blocked by a mysterious dark haired man pulling a gun out of his jacket. She started backpedaling in horror.

"Get down!" the dark haired man said as he pushed Jen to the ground and shot the man in the doorway. He fired again hitting the man at the counter in the shoulder. The wounded man dropped to the floor using Frank as a shield. Jen's rescuer loosed off two more shots while he overturned a table and pulled Jen behind it. Two more men had come through the back door, guns drawn, seeking cover behind the counter.

The man behind the table with Jen turned to her and asked, "Are you okay? Are you hit?"

"I think so. I mean, I think I'm okay."

"Hold that thought."

The dark haired man leaned around the table and fired at the new arrivals. One was hit in the chest, and the other returned fire blindly, hitting nothing.

Ducking back behind the table,

the dark haired man called out, "Hey, Frank!"

The injured man behind Frank pulled him closer, causing them both to flinch.

"Yeah?"

"How you holding up?"

Frank looked at his raw and bloody hands with a couple of missing fingernails.

"Just peachy."

"Frank?"

"What?"

"I got the girl."

"Good for you." Frank said, trying to keep the frustration out of his voice.

The two men in suits looked at each other in disbelief.

Jen was also looking at the stranger behind the table in confusion.

The man behind the counter took a shot at the overturned table.

"Do you mind? I'm trying to have a conversation here." said the dark haired man as he sent a couple of shots of cover fire back. The man in the suit ducked behind the counter, and the dark haired man loaded a fresh magazine.

"So, Frank, what's the plan?"

"Oh, you know, save the girl, save

the world. But what I would really like is for you to quit fucking around!" Frank felt he was losing the battle to keep desperation out of his voice.

Suddenly, Franks' captor spoke up.

"Hey, asshole! Throw your gun over here or I'm going to shoot your boyfriend in the head!"

"Frank?"

"I could really use your help. Do what you gotta do."

As the dark haired man turned to take aim at his attackers, Jen grabbed his arm, with a concerned look on her face.

"Wait, what if you hit Frank?"

"I always hit what I aim at."

"You're sure?"

"Of course I am."

The dark haired man rose from behind the table, crouched on one knee, and fired, hitting Frank in the middle of the forehead. As Frank slumped, in death, the dark haired man managed to shoot the man holding Frank, killing him as well. He ducked back behind the table.

"Oops."

Jen was horrified; the dark haired man shrugged apologetically. He rose up again and managed to shoot the man behind the counter. The dark haired man stood up and turned to Jen.

"You need to come with me."

He noticed the man behind the counter, crawling toward the back door. He raised his pistol, as Jen grabbed his arm.

"Who are you? Who are they? What's going on?"

"I'm Sam, they're the bad guys. Now decide, come with me and live, or stay here and die."

"What about the cops? Someone will have called them."

"Do you want to explain this to the cops?"

Jen looked at the carnage, and came to a decision.

"What are you waiting for? Let's go!"

Sam turned back to the man who was heading for the door and saw him trying to take aim. Sam shot from the hip and killed him.

Jen frantically ran from the cafe, while Sam walked calmly. He caught up to her and slowed her down to a normal pace.

"Don't run. We don't want to draw attention to ourselves."

"Are you kidding me? What about that gunfight? People are going to notice."

"That's true, but if we walk, people won't know we were involved. We run, and our descriptions will be going out to every law enforcement agency. Don't freak out, just act normal. We'll take my car."

"How do I know it's safe to go with you?"

"I shot the guys who were shooting at you. That ought to give you a hint."

As Sam and Jen rounded the corner to the back parking lot, Sam clicked the button on his remote starter and his car blew up. They were unhurt by the blast, but were in need of transportation.

"Change of plans." Sam said as they turned back and rounded another corner. "Hail that cab. Now!"

Jen hailed the cab and it stopped. They got in. The driver's accented voice carried from the front.

"Howdy folks, where to?"

"Just drive" Sam replied, "we'll tell you where to go later."

"Suit yourself. As long as meter running, you are boss."

After a couple of blocks, the driver finally spoke.

"So, are you two newlyweds? You

look like newlyweds. All nervous together for the first time."

"We're not married." Jen responded, then added, "We just met."

"Ah, first date jitters. Have no fear, you're in good hands. Bernie will make sure date goes smooth like milk."

"Who's Bernie?" Sam asked, looking over the front seat to the license on the dash.

"That's me. I'm Bernie."

"That's not the name on your license."

"Bernie is not my real name, of course, but I think all cabbies should be called Bernie. Is good cabbie name, don't you think? It helps make ride more romantic."

"Well, hello Bernie. I'm Jen and this is Sam. Of course, those may not be our real names either."

"Ah yes, mystery and intrigue! Add to romance, yes? If you don't mind me saying, you two make cute couple."

Jen started laughing uncontrollably, which eventually turned into sobbing.

In a vacant parking garage, Eddie, the security supervisor for Lassiter International Enterprises, lay face up, with a knife in his belly. A pair of Nitrile gloved hands searched his pockets and pulled out a wallet. The searcher placed it on Eddie's chest. Next, his watch was removed, and after a quick pat down for any other valuables, a ring was slipped from a fat finger, and placed with the wallet and watch. A plastic bag, was produced from a jacket pocket and all items placed inside, along with the knife which was jerked from the body. Stan looked down at the corpse.

"Sorry, Eddie." was all he said before walking to the exit.

Bernie had been observing Jen as she tried to compose herself.

"I say something bad?"

"She's just had a rough day." Sam replied.

Looking at Jen through the rear-view, Bernie said, "You tell Bernie your troubles."

"You don't want to know." Sam said.

"You listen to me. Talking helps. I'm very good listener."

"You'd never believe it."

"I be the judge. You say."

"Would you believe some bad men

slaughtered her friends and co-workers and were going to kill her when I showed up and saved her?"

"For serious?"

"Sure. For serious."

Bernie contemplated what he had just heard for half of a block.

"I believe."

"Why?" Jen asked. "The story sounds ridiculous."

"Today, crazy day; just this morning, I pick up fare who say, "Just drive, I tell you where later." Then, he say, "Pull over." Next thing you know, he run, like crazy person into building. Then, he run like crazy person out of building, take another cab and go back the way we came. That driver not so good as me. He no pay attention and Boom! He have an accident. Now, you say same thing, "Just drive, I tell you where later." After what I see, crazy don't seem so crazy today. At least it's no boring."

"That's a bit of a coincidence." Sam said, suspicious. "Why did you come back?"

"No coincidence. This my territory. If two people take cab in this neighborhood, I gonna be driver they get, most every time. Any crazy, in this neighborhood, is bad

for business. I may not be fancy-
pants big shot, but I still
important. Now, you tell me, why
people shoot at you?"

"Who said they were shooting?"

"I heard gunshots. Too much
coincidence that people try to kill
you and I hear gunshots. Must be
shooting at you. Is also why I
believe you."

Jen looked at Sam, "I told you."

"Why should we tell a random
stranger about any of this?" Jen
asked Bernie.

"Who better than random
stranger? Only people who know you
try to kill you."

"Look Bernie, no offense," Sam
said, "We really can't say any more
without putting you in danger."

"I'm no stranger to danger. Get
it? Rhyming all the timing I am.
Look, Maybe-Jen-and-Sam-maybe-not-
Jen-and-Sam, you seem nice couple.
If you bad people, you already shoot
me. You no shoot me, so must be good
people in trouble. You need help,
you call me. You take my card, I
take you serious. Good?"

Bernie took a card, from his
pocket, and handed it to Jen.

"Good." Jen replied.

Looking in the mirror at Sam,

he asked, "Good?"

"Fine. Good."

"Good! Now, where we go?"

"I don't know." Jen replied.

"We're going to her place."

"What? No, absolutely not! You're not bringing this insanity to my place."

"I'm open to suggestions." Sam said.

"Not to buttinski, but what about coffee shop up ahead?"

"Thanks, Bernie." Jen replied, "That will do just fine."

"Sure, as long as it's okay with Bernie." Sam said with a bit of sour grapes.

Bernie pulled to the curb in front of the coffee shop, got out and opened the door for Jen and Sam. He then went around and opened the coffee shop door for Jen.

"Special service for special lady. Remember, you get to trouble, you call Bernie. You Jen, call any time. You Sam, not so much."

Sam paid Bernie and walked inside the building, dismissing the cab driver.

"Want anything?" Sam asked, trying to appear normal.

"An explanation?" Jen replied impatiently.

Sam did not answer.

"Fine, something mocha."

"Grab a seat over there, try to relax and I'll get the coffee."

"I'm going to the bathroom."

Jen walked to the bathroom, while Sam placed the order and tried to make nonchalant small talk. Sam was keeping an eye on the front door, but from her vantage point, the barista could see the back door, and Jen sneaking out.

CHAPTER 38

The two men wore black suits and blue Nitrile gloves. As former police investigators, they knew exactly what would be looked for, and what would be over-looked. This was not the first time they had staged a household "accident". More people die in their homes than on the highways, statistically speaking. Anne Banner, computer tech for Lassiter International Enterprises, would be just another statistic, who slipped and hit her head getting out of the bathtub.

'What the hell is taking her so long?', Sam thought to himself, while he sat at the table drinking coffee. The place was not that big, she could not be at a different table waiting for him. He eventually sauntered back toward the ladies room; maybe she was having another breakdown. He listened at the door, but heard no weeping, flushing, or even running water. Perplexed, he opened the door and poked his head inside; the room was completely empty. No feet under the stall doors, nothing. Backing out of the small hallway, Sam noticed the rear exit.

"Shit", he muttered under his breath, rushing out the door.

Jen felt herself starting to feel safe as the cab pulled up in front of her apartment building. She supposed it was some kind of instinct, or a response to familiar surroundings. She knew she was not safe because there were people out there trying to kill her, for reasons only they knew. She was not sure where she would go, but she knew she had to get out of town, and that meant changing out of her work clothes and packing a bag.

"Thanks for getting me, Bernie. Would you mind waiting for me while I pack?"

"Are you sure about leaving Sam behind?"

"I'll be safer on my own. Promise me you'll wait."

"For you, anything."

Jen smiled at that and went in to the apartment building. She unlocked the door to her unit, turned off the alarm, turned on the light, and headed to the bedroom. She pulled off her work clothes, and started making a mental packing list. Suitcase: under the bed. Underwear and socks: in the dresser, along with t-shirts. Pants and a jacket: in the closet, right behind the man in the hat with the gun.

She stifled a scream, when he stepped out of her closet, and pointed his pistol at her chest. He gave her a slow once over, admiring her bra and panties.

"Don't stop on my account, love." he said in a thick cockney accent.

"Please don't hurt me." was all Jen could stammer; her brain and instincts fought to either cover her state of undress, hold still so the man would not shoot her, or run for her life.

"Wouldn't dream of it, would we, Tommy?"

Jen turned away from the closet man, to see another taller man blocking her bedroom door.

"No. Not a bit, Nigel."

The man blocking the door had a more cultured British accent, Jen noticed. Tommy walked to the closet, and pulled a pair of blue jeans off a hanger. Together with a t-shirt, he had fished from her dresser, he tossed them to Jen.

"Here, put these on."

Jen caught them and tried to rationalize what was going on.

"Unless", the man continued, "of

course, you wish to continue this conversation in the all together. I certainly don't mind. Nigel, would you mind putting the kettle on?"

Nigel did mind, but went to the kitchen. Business before pleasure, all for queen and country. Tommy moved back by the door. Jen stared at him, expecting him to turn his head or avert his eyes.

"Do you mind?", she finally asked.

"Not at all."

"A little privacy, please?"

"I'm afraid that won't do. Dress!"

Nigel, clearly annoyed, burst past his partner and addressed Jen.

"Is this all you have?"

Jen looked up at him and saw that he was holding her box of generic brand tea bags.

"Uh, yes. I might have some coffee, but it's instant. I drink more tea than coffee."

Nigel rolled his eyes in frustration.

"Philistines.", he said to Jen before turning to his partner.

"Can't get a decent cuppa in this country."

"Now, now, Nigel. When in Rome, be a good chap and make do."

Nigel left the room, muttering.

As Jen finished dressing, Tommy gestured for her to lead the way back into the living room.

CHAPTER 39

Street lights threw shadows across the darkened diner, the yellow Crime Scene tape took on an eerie glow. Two men walked down the street, dressed in blue jeans, cowboy boots, western shirts and leather fringe jackets. Seeing the tape, they could not resist peering in the dark windows; just human nature.

Two men wearing NSA wind breakers, had just stepped from the diner doorway, at the same time that the leather jackets were peeking. One of the wind breakers approached the other two, a mix of Harry Nilson and Tex Ritter suddenly playing in his head. He pulled his I.D., which informed anyone not behind him, that he was agent Brown with the National Security Agency.

"NSA. This area is off limits. You need to move along, now."

The short cowboy stepped forward and spoke, his western twang completing the look.

"Sorry there officer, we was just curious is all. What went on here?"

Brown's partner, agent Greene, stepped forward.

"I'm sorry, we can't discuss the case. You need to move on."

"Aw, c'mon, we heard on the news there was a big ol' shoot-em-up here. Kinda like the OK Corral."

"That's right, and we've been sifting through the site looking for clues." Agent Brown responded, and noticing a glare from his partner, continued, "Now, I've asked you politely, please leave before we have you hauled in for obstruction."

Unexpectedly, the tall cowboy asked in a thick Russian accent.

"Do you find anything?"

Brown and Greene looked at each other, and then suspiciously, back to the cowboys.

"Where are you from?" inquired agent Greene.

The short one spoke up quickly.

"Don't mind him none. We hail from Nebraska."

Brown and Greene exchanged another look and the two cowboys did the same. In a flash of microseconds, all four moved for the weapons under their jackets. The cowboys won the quick-draw competition, and the two NSA agents dropped in their tracks. The tall one turned to his partner, and in Russian, stated,

"We need information. We must check in."

"And these two?" the short one replied, also in Russian, and gesturing annoyedly to the two conspicuous bodies on the sidewalk.

"Leave them."

"I regret the day I met you.", the short one replied; they continued walking down the sidewalk.

CHAPTER 40

For Nigel Black, working with MI6 had given him several stimulating challenges. Over the years, he had traveled to distant lands, handled government secrets, and even guarded heads of state. He thought about these moments as he was stuck serving tea to his partner and a civilian waitress. She had neither decent tea nor proper condiments. How was she expected to be of use in the search for this chip? Nigel set the tray with the pot and cups on a small table next to Tommy.

"All I could find was two percent."

"I'll do without."

Turning to Jen, on the couch, Tommy asked, "Tea?"

Jen just shook her head no.

Tommy accepted the cup from Nigel and then continued,

"Do you know what I find most irritating about America?"

Jen looked at him, uncertain what to say so she just shook her head again.

"The dishonesty. You people have royalty, but never admit it to anyone, even to yourselves. Take this current situation. Nigel and I are here because a businessman, not a senator or a judge, a businessman, is in trouble. His company developed a virus that can wipe out all computer technology indiscriminately, and then he lost it. The NSA is here, the Russians, God help us, and who knows who else, all because this man Lassiter lost this Wildfire gubbins. The man's actions move nations and you still insist he's not royalty just because he doesn't have a crown."

"I have no idea what you're talking about." Jen said, breaking her silence. "What has any of this got to do with me?"

Nigel Black had reached his limit. Setting his cup down, in two strides, he approached the couch, and gave Jen a vicious backhanded slap across the face. Grabbing the front of her t-shirt, he pulled her upright and leaned in, close.

"Quit playin' dumb, sunshine."

Tommy made no move to get up, simply raised his voice slightly.

"Now, now, Nigel. There's no call to be uncivilized. Yet."

Looking at Jen, he asked,

"Where's the chip, dear?"

Nigel released Jen and went back to the table and continued to drink his tea.

"I've never heard of anything called Wildfire." Jen's voice trembled a little as the words poured out. "You've got the wrong person. I'm just a waitress."

Tommy looked over at his partner.

"Oh dear, she's a bit thick, isn't she, Nigel?"

Nigel nodded as Tommy leaned toward Jen, his manner of speech was slow and deliberate.

"You waited on Frank Emerson today. Frank stole the chip. Frank gave you the chip. Now, you need to give us the chip so we can all go home."

Jen wondered if they knew Frank was dead. She thought about saying something, but did not want to give them any ideas.

"Frank didn't give me anything. I swear."

"Well then, there's no reason to keep you alive, is there?"

'Apparently they don't need me to give them that idea', thought Jen. The words were music to Nigel's ears, and his hand was in his pocket, fingers wrapped around a knife as he advanced toward the couch.

"More tea, please, Nigel.",
Tommy chimed in, breaking the
tension. Disappointment crossed his
face, as Nigel released the grip of
his knife and picked up the tray. He
was not sure what his partner had in
mind, but he had agreed to follow
Tommy's lead.

Jen knew her time was short. If
she did not do something soon, these
two Limey assholes were going to
kill her. She hoped that the cab was
still waiting downstairs. Seeing
that the two men were distracted
with their tea and trying to plan
their next move, Jen gathered her
courage and bolted for the door.

She took four steps before
Nigel intercepted her and grabbed a
handful of her hair. Using her
momentum against her, he slammed her
head-first into the wall. She
crumpled, dazedly, against the wall,
her hands up defensively.

Leaning down, Nigel grabbed the
hair on top of her head and forced
her face up, knocking the back of
her head against the wall.

"Not so fast, you little bitch!"
he snarled.

Tommy was also standing over
her now, his voice was still calm.

"I realize you're most likely a
pawn in this game. The only choice

left you is to play your part. One last time, where is the chip?"

Jen's head was ringing, but she knew he was right, her only choice was to play along.

"It's...it's at the cafe. I'll show you where."

"That's my good girl." Tommy said as he extended a hand to help her up.

Nigel was first to leave the apartment building, followed by Jen, and Tommy behind her. Jen's eyes searched, frantically, for Bernie, but he was nowhere. 'Damn', she thought, 'I should've left a better tip. Maybe he had a local call, maybe he thought he'd be quick enough to make it before I finished packing. Maybe the police know about the diner and are there already'. As the list of hopeful maybes ran through her head, she heard the sound of a car engine racing.

Suddenly, in front of Nigel Black, twin headlights appeared, momentarily blinding him. The screech of tires was followed by a dull thump, and Nigel flew five feet, through the air, the building breaking his fall, among other things.

Jen, quick to take advantage of the chaos, elbowed Tommy in the solar plexus, knocking the wind out of him. She started running.

Sam came running from the shadows, to deliver the coup de gras to Tommy, and left him where he fell. Moving to Nigel, Sam noticed he was still breathing. A quick stomp to the throat fixed that problem.

Meanwhile, Bernie had emerged from his cab, and was trying to comfort Jen.

"You alright?"

"I think so. Just a little bruised, maybe."

Sam walked over to them.

"Still think you can survive without me?"

"It's still early." Jen replied, "How can I possibly trust you? Every time I see you, you end up killing someone."

"Does it count that they were trying to kill you?"

"Is true.", Bernie chimed in, trying to point out Sam's logic to Jen.

"So, do you know what they were after?" Sam asked, trying to get back on topic.

"Yeah, it was something called Wildfire. Only, I don't have it."

"Then where were you going?"

"Back to the diner. I was playing for time, hoping I'd find a way to escape. I thought I might get a message to Bernie to call the cops or something."

"Speaking of which," Sam turned his attention to Bernie, "Can you give me a hand with these bodies?"

Bernie looked at both bodies, as he made the sign of the cross.

"Where we take them?"

Sam grabbed Nigel, by the shoulders, and was indicating for Bernie to grab the dead man's feet.

"We'll just put them in the trash with the other one."

"Other one?!" Bernie and Jen said simultaneously.

"Yeah, I killed Jen's stalker this morning."

Bernie looked at Sam, with a re-appraising eye.

"I'm thinking you're not such good person as I thought."

"Believe me, Bern, it had to be done. Now grab that end."

Bernie muttered under his breath, as he picked up the feet. While they hid the bodies, Jen paced nervously, eventually finding herself in the back of the cab, sunk low in the seat, hoping to disappear.

CHAPTER 41

A short time later, they were all in the cab traveling to what Sam hoped was a safe house.

"I'll never be safe, will I?" Jen asked, staring blankly out the window.

"No." Sam replied flatly, "You're pretty much screwed."

"Why were they looking for me? I don't know anything."

"Frank sent me a text with your picture and a coded message telling me he gave you the chip. They probably got your picture from his phone. What I want to know is, how did British Intelligence find out about Wildfire?"

This re-focused Jen's attention.

"They're spies, it's what they do. Plus, they're our allies, why wouldn't they know?"

"Because Wildfire would screw everybody, allies and enemies alike."

"Then why build it?"

"Bureaucrats are idiots. They make decisions based on politics and money, and don't consider the consequences. They wanted a computer virus that couldn't be blocked, so

Frank designed it without limitations. When he succeeded, he realized it was too powerful to entrust to anyone. That's when he brought me in, to help him steal it."

"Well, Frank didn't give me anything remotely like a computer chip."

"You're sure?"

"Yes" Jen said, irritated. "I'm sure."

"Fine." Sam replied, "You have to promise me you won't try to run away again."

"Why?" Jen asked, suspicion creeping into her voice.

"Because I think Lassiter has implemented Order Eighty-six. If that's the case, you're going to need all the help you can get."

"What's Order Eighty-six?"

"Just what the name implies. An attempt to put the genie back in the bottle. If you're not part of The Wildfire Initiative, you get eighty-sixed. It doesn't matter if you have the chip, you're targeted for elimination by some very nasty people."

"So how are you going to get me out of this?"

"I'm still working on it." Sam turned his gaze to the front seat.

"Sorry, Bernie, but you're a target as well now. You both know too much."

"Now I understand why they say, 'No good deed goes unpunished'. We are nearing destination, are you sure is safe?"

"We have to risk it. Pull behind the building. We'll go in the back."

They pulled around back of a two story building, and parked the cab in the shadows near the street lights. Up a flight of stairs, Sam unlocked a room the size of a small studio apartment. There was a table and two chairs in one corner, and a small bookshelf with a portable television on top in another. Next to the bookshelf was a dorm fridge. Papers were scattered over every flat surface.

Jen appraised the room, after Sam had turned on the overhead light.

"Looks like someone's searched this place already."

"Naw, it always looks like this."

Jen and Bernie exchange a look as, Sam walked over to the bookshelf and pulled out an envelope hidden behind it. The envelope was addressed to Julius Rosenberg.

"Here it is." Sam announced,

holding the envelope for all to see. He opened it and extracted a thick metal ring. He gave it a quick inspection before removing a note.

"Well?" Jen asked expectantly as Sam read the note.

Sam held up the metal ring, still looking at the note.

"This doodad is the key to the treasure, according to this note."

Thinking back on Frank's text, he absently muttered,

"What do treasure maps have in common?"

Bernie, standing close enough to hear him, exclaimed, "X marks spot!"

Sam examined the metal ring more closely, turning it over in his hands. A look of recognition came into his eyes. "I know what this is."

Looking at Jen, he asked, "Did Frank leave you a tip?"

"Of course. He was a nice guy, unlike some."

"What did you do with it?" Sam asked, ignoring the slant.

"I traded the coins for bills and put the rest in my change jar at home."

"This is old school spy stuff." Sam said, holding the metal ring out for Jen and Bernie to see. "This ring opens a hollow coin. Frank gave you the chip hidden inside a coin!"

This time, it was Jen who had the revelation.

"I know the one you mean."

"Where is it now?" asked Sam.

"Uh, I took it with me to the audition. I think it's back at my apartment."

"You didn't change it at the diner?"

"No, it was a half dollar. I held on to it for luck."

"So we go back to your apartment."

"It's not safe at my apartment. I've already been attacked there once."

"Yeah, but this time you'll have backup."

Jen looked to Bernie, who shrugged, then to Sam, then back to Bernie. Throwing up her hands in surrender, she walked out of the room, followed by Bernie, and Sam turned out the lights and locked the door.

They piled into the cab, and pulled away from the curb, heading back to Jen's apartment. Another car pulled away from the same curb, half a block down.

A few blocks later, Sam asked,

"Hey Bernie, can you lose our tail?"

"I thought you'd never ask. They eat my dusty shorts."

Jen turned around and saw twin headlights coming around a corner they just turned.

"Please to excuse Sam, do you have gun?"

"Yes, why?" Sam replied with an air of caution.

"Good." was all Bernie said, "I have plan."

"What's the plan?" Sam inquired.

Bernie reached under the seat, and pulled out a revolver.

"Oh my God, Bernie!" Jen exclaimed, "Where did you get that?"

"Is protection. Is first time I need it."

"So what's the plan?" Sam asked again, with some edge in his voice.

"Not to worry, leave to me. I fix."

In the backseat, a concerned Jen turned to her fellow passenger.

"Uh, Sam?"

Sam looked at her and shrugged.

"Trust me. Sam, you cover, yes?"

Sam unholstered his gun.

"Sure, why not? So, for the third time. What's. The. Plan?"

"Hang on." Bernie said as he stomped on the brakes, stopping the cab. He then put the cab in reverse, aiming for the trailing car. He stopped short of hitting the car, as it came to a panicked stop.

"Wait here, please." was all Bernie said, to the backseat, as he exited, leaving his door ajar. He calmly walked toward the other car, with his hands behind his back and a big smile. He paused at the rear of the cab, and leaned over as if he was looking for something.

Standing upright, he smiled and waved cheerily to the two men in the car. Confused, the nodded and waved back. Bernie then stepped further away from both vehicles, as if to get a better perspective. He whipped out the gun and shot the front tire of the tailing car. He then ran back to the cab and jumped in the drivers seat. Shifting into drive, he sped to the next corner and turned, as the two men emerged from their car. One goon was inspecting the tire, while the other chased the cab on foot; he gave up when the cab disappeared around the corner.

In the front seat, Bernie was proud. In the back, Sam was fuming and Jen laughed.

"That was hysterical. Did you see the look on their faces?"

"Are you out of your mind? You

could have gotten us killed." Sam said, directing his anger toward the front seat.

"Oh, lighten up. Everyone's been trying to kill us all day." said Jen.

"Sam is right." Bernie said, collecting himself. "Was big risk."

Jen's laughter subsided, as she considered the seriousness of their situation.

"Very serious business." Bernie continued, before adding, "But still fun."

Bernie and Jen both laugh this time, but Sam is still angry.

"Sam, you were right." Jen said, catching her breath, "with backup like you guys, I've got nothing to worry about."

Jen started laughing again, and even Sam could not help a smile; they drove on through the night.

CHAPTER 42

Bernie pulled up in front of Jen's apartment building and parked.

"You two go, I keep good lookout."

"Thank you, Bernie." Jen said. "You're a doll."

"I blushing doll. Go, before I decide Sam not good for you."

"Screw you, Bernie." Sam commented from the backseat, the quietly added, "And thanks."

"See", Bernie said, meeting Sam's gaze in the rear view, "You learning. Not so much the schmuck, now."

Sam and Jen left the cab and entered the apartment building; Bernie scanned the street for any signs of life.

Entering her apartment, Jen went to her change jar and started sifting through coins.

"Frank paid for his coffee with change and over tipped me. At the time, I thought he was just trying to make an impression, but I found a coin with an x marked on it. I thought it was odd and I was going to keep it for luck, but I finally ended up putting it in here with the rest of my loose change."

Sam looked around the room and noticed, a coin on a small table next to the answering machine.

"Is this it?" he asked, holding it up.

She looked replying, "No, this one's different."

Jen thought for a moment, and then realization crossed her face.

"I've got it."

She ran back to her bedroom and rummaged through her discarded work clothes, finally unearthing the coin from her apron pocket. Moving back into the living room, she held the coin up, triumphantly.

"See? X marks the spot. On a silver coin, just like a treasure map. Actually, I was rubbing the coin for luck before the audition and wiped most of the x off."

She rubbed the remaining ink off with her thumb and showed Sam the smudge.

"See?"

Jen handed the coin to Sam; he examined it closely before fishing the metal ring out of his pocket. Putting the coin into the ring, he slapped it into his open palm; the coin separated, revealing the Wildfire chip. They both stared, mesmerized, at the contents of his hand.

"This is it. Plug this into any computer and it'll set off a chain reaction that will ruin the world as we know it."

"What do we do now?" Jen asked, turning her gaze from his hand to his face.

"What do you think we should do?" Sam replied, meeting her gaze.

"Destroy it, duh!"

"that's not as easy as it seems. The coding is hard wired, so a magnet won't erase it. We need to physically destroy it in a way that it can't be rebuilt or reverse engineered. That means melting it down and these babies are tempered to handle a lot of heat."

"Fine." Jen said flatly, "Then we plug it into my laptop and let it do its thing."

"Are you kidding me?!" Sam asked, scanning her face for any sign of mirth...or insanity.

"Why not? Mankind can live without computers. We got along just fine without them for thousands of years. And, if the virus is released, no one will have any reason to come after me anymore, right?"

"True," he said, momentarily

distracted; "but, think about what you're suggesting. Everything is digitized. Everything that is computerized would have to be switched to manual. In some cases, the manual infrastructure doesn't even exist anymore. It would be chaos."

"So people will have to adjust, that's all. Education would be important again. Libraries have books for all we need to know. It'll be tough at first, but people will get through it. Give me the chip."

Jen reached a hand towards his; he recoiled out of instinct.

"Do you realize what you're doing?" Sam asked, again searching her face.

"I do. Give me the chip." she replied, again, reaching her hand out.

"Once it's done, we can't take it back. Think about it."

"Just give me the damn chip." Jen said, and took the chip and coin halves from his hand. Sam stared, dumbfounded, as she reassembled the three pieces.

"There. We hold onto it until we can decide what to do with it. You are such a dumb-ass." Jen was smiling.

"Maybe it would be better if you let me hold on to that." Sam said, still a little mistrustful.

Jen considered for a moment, and then tossed a coin to him.

"Sure." she said, and headed to the couch.

"You are one bizarrely strange girl." Sam said; he started casually pacing the length of the room.

"No offense taken."

"None intended." Sam said, pausing in front of her and holding up the coin.

"This is our only leverage." Sam started as he pocketed the coin and ring. "If we destroy it, there's nothing to keep them from killing you just for knowing about it."

"I'm aware, you know." She recalled their earlier exchange. "I've heard rumors that the missiles will launch if they don't get confirmation that the world still exists. I don't know if that's true or not, but my life isn't worth risking it."

She turned her attention to Sam, who had resumed pacing.

"Is it true? Will the missiles launch if they don't get a signal?"

"Hell if I know." Sam answered, distracted. "The government treats me like a mushroom. They keep me in the dark and feed me a lot of shit."

Pausing to face her, he said, "I told you I'm not going to let anything happen to you and I mean it. Now, we just need to figure our next move."

At that moment, the crash of splintering wood and the front door hitting the wall filled the room, startling Jen and Sam. A second later, the crash of breaking glass, as one of Jen's patio chairs shattered the sliding door.

Through both broken doors, two men, dressed in dark clothes, with hoods pulled down tightly on their heads entered Jen's apartment.

In one continuous motion, Sam pushed Jen over the couch, drew his pistol, turned, and fired at the man coming through the front door. The guy ducked and the bullet whizzed past his head. The man at the slider fired, wounding Sam, who then lunged at the man, both of them falling backward.

Bernie heard the breaking glass from the cab's front seat. As he got out to investigate, and render assistance, a short man wearing a balaclava hit him from behind with a blackjack. Bernie crumpled to the ground.

"Wiesz, hol ihn!" called the front door man. Hearing nothing, he advanced, gun drawn. Jen's fight or flight instinct took over; she rolled back over the couch and went to the small table where she kept her magic props.

Rounding the corner, the hooded man was greeted with a rubber thumb bouncing off his forehead, momentarily distracting him. Jen threw a silk scarf over his head, knocked him off balance, and drove him into the corner. Kicking and clawing, she managed to wrestle the gun out of his hand, and then cuff his hand to the same pipe that had held her captive earlier that morning.

The hooded man looked at his predicament, then at Jen, standing in front of him, holding his gun by the barrel. Reaching up with his free hand, the man released the trick handcuff, stood up, and grabbed for his gun in Jen's hand. She put up a good fight but ultimately, the scary guy won. He raised it, took aim, and was knocked back by two shots to the chest. Jen turned around, and saw Sam holding a smoking gun.

Sam winced in pain standing up and faced Jen.

"It helps if you don't let him take the gun back, Hermione."

"Shut up." was all Jen said.

CHAPTER 43

When the adrenaline started to wear off, Jen felt her knuckles throb, where she had hit the hooded man. She flexed and massaged it, even thought about putting ice on it, but her feet just kept wandering around the room, while her head tried to make sense of what had happened.

"Was that German? It sounded like he was speaking German."

"I don't know, might have been Russian. Doesn't matter. It definitely means other governments are involved now,"

Jen turned to face him, about to say something, when she noticed a blood stain, barely visible under his jacket.

"Oh my God, you're bleeding."

Sam looked down and noticed the stain.

"Huh, so I am."

"Take your jacket off, let me see."

"I'm sure I'll be okay. It doesn't hurt that bad."

"Are you in shock?" she asked, stepped forward, and slapped him in the face.

"No, I felt that."

"I have a first aid kit in the bathroom. Take your jacket off and try to stay alert."

Jen left and retrieved the kit.

"Come over here by the light and lift up your shirt."

"Aw, shucks, I'll bet you say that to all the boys.", Sam said as he followed her to a lamp by the couch.

"So, what's this about these other governments?" Jen asked as she started tending his wound.

"You don't understand, it's too soon. A leak was inevitable, but not this fast."

"Maybe those were more of Lassiter's men."

"No way. First the Brits and now the Germans. No, these guys were ahead of Lassiter, which means they are fully informed and operational."

Jen dabbed a cotton ball with antiseptic on Sam's wound.

"Ow! Take it easy, it's just a scratch."

"Sorry." Jen said, looking up at him.

The phone rang.

"Don't answer that." Sam said.

"Why not?"

"It's probably Lassiter." Sam

said with some joviality in his voice.

"Yeah, right. The head of the spy ring trying to kill me is going to call me up and ask to meet. It's probably just my agent."

Picking up the phone, Jen asked, "Hello?"

"Hello Jennifer, my name is Lassiter. I think it's about time we meet to discuss returning my property."

Jen dropped the phone, like it had bitten her, and sat down wide-eyed, on the couch.

The phone, on the floor, still had Lassiter's voice coming from it.

"Hello?...Hello?"

Jen pointed at the phone, and in a sharp whisper to Sam said, "It's him!"

"Who?" Sam whispered back.

"Lassiter!" Jen whispered, "Lassiter is on the phone! Right now!"

Sam reached down, and picked up the phone, putting it to his ear.

"Hi there, Lassie. How's tricks?"

"Samuel. You're still alive. I thought you might have been killed in that unfortunate incident at the cafe."

"No such luck."

"Do you have my property?"

"I know where I can get my hands on it. I know more than that, though, you have a mouse in your house."

"I beg your pardon?"

"I just killed a couple of guys who didn't act like your usual Keystone clods. They were speaking German."

He raised his shoulders and made a quizzical look at Jen, who shrugged back and nodded.

"Are you sure?" Lassiter asked.

"I've got it on good authority, it was German, or possibly Russian."

"Try to make sense, Samuel."

"The point is, they weren't from around here. Who knows the chip has gone missing?"

"Presumably, no one. We've handled anyone who might have come into contact with Mister Emerson."

"I'm sure you have. That begs the question, how did these guys find out?" Doing his best Ricky Ricardo impression, he added, "Lassie, you've got some 'splainin' to do."

"Well, Samuel, if what you're telling me is true, we do indeed have some topics to discuss. Do you remember the warehouse?"

"I know the one you mean."

"Meet me there in one hour, and bring my property."

"I'll be there with bells on, Lassie."

"Would you mind terribly not calling me that, Samuel?"

"Yes, I would mind, Lassie."

Sam disconnected the call.

"Asshole." Sam muttered, half under his breath.

"What did he say?" Jen asked.

"He wants the chip. He isn't sure you know anything about it, but he's sure you have it, or he wouldn't have called here. So we'll meet him, and when he asks to see the chip, you distract him and I'll shoot him."

"That is the dumbest plan ever."

"What's wrong with it?"

"I'd prefer a plan where I live long enough to say I told you so."

"Well, we're going with my plan, unless you can conjure up a few white tigers to take him out."

Jen walked to and removed a jacket from the closet.

"Are you familiar with the ending of Butch Cassidy and The Sundance Kid?", Sam asked.

"Where the two of them are gunned down by the Mexican army?"

"Bolivian, actually. Historically, they survived that fight. They weren't killed until much later."

"Gee, I feel so much better. What's your point?"

"No point, it just popped into my head is all."

"You're weird. Ready?"

"Let's go."

Sam ushered Jen out the door, and glanced back at the tornado-ed apartment.

"Better call a maid service." he said; he turned off the light, and closed the broken door as best he could.

Walking out of the building, Sam whistled a familiar Englebert Humperdink tune that Jen could not quite place. She noticed Bernie laying on the ground, next to his cab. Sam's whistling stopped abruptly.

"Bernie!" Jen called out, "Sam, we have to do something." Looking past his shoulder, she yelled, "Look out!"

Four men, in black suits, grabbed Sam and Jen, pinned their arms to their sides, and restrained their wrists. Cloth bags were put over their heads. They struggled as the men dragged them to separate vehicles, leaving Bernie's still form behind, lying in a pool of blood.

CHAPTER 44

Jen had no idea how long she had been in the dark. She remembered resisting restraint, being shoved roughly into a vehicle, and driven for probably thirty minutes in silence. Then she was removed and dragged somewhere to be put in a chair and tied to it.

When the cloth bag was finally removed, all she could see was blinding light with darkness just beyond. As her eyes grew accustomed to the light, she saw Sam in the same predicament about four feet away. A voice spoke from the darkness.

"Welcome to the warehouse, Samuel."

"What's with the kidnapping, Lassie? We were on our way here to meet you."

"Yes, but I assumed you had some sort of plan to distract and then shoot me, so I decided an escort would be best. It's for the safety of all concerned."

Jen looked over at Sam.

"I told you it was a bad plan."

"Well, you got to say, I told you so. Happy now?"

"Not really."

A well dressed, middle-aged man with short cropped graying hair and mustache stepped into the light. As he walked up to Jen, she realized this was the face behind the voice.

"We haven't been properly introduced. Charles Lassiter, at your service."

" Charmed, I'm sure."

"I apologize, but I never bothered to learn your full name."

"You can just go on calling me Dead Meat. I'm sure that's what you've been calling me ever since the spy master here walked into my life." she said, nodding her head toward Sam.

Looking at Sam, Lassiter said, "I like her, she's got spunk." Turning his gaze back to Jen, he continued, "I will truly regret your passing."

"Why don't you let her go." Sam protested, "She doesn't know anything. She just got sucked into this because she happened to wait on Frank's table."

"Whatever she may or may not have known earlier is of little consequence. She knows entirely too much now."

"If you don't let her go, I

won't help you find the leak in your security."

"That's right, there's a mouse in my house. Who talks like that, really? You've been watching too many spy movies, Samuel."

"Oh, come on, dad, give me a break."

"Dad!" Jen could not believe what she just heard. "Dad?!"

Lassiter turned his attention back to Jen.

"I see he has not been entirely forthcoming with you. Meet my son, Samuel Lassiter. He always wanted to be a spy, but when he got the chance, he failed to meet their requirements. Something of a disappointment, really. But the disappointments will end soon, as I mourn the passing of the late Samuel Lassiter."

"You're going to kill your own son?" Jen said in astonishment.

"It's a lot less paperwork than disowning him."

"I told you he was an asshole." Sam said.

"Frank and Samuel were college roommates where they used to play out their little spy fantasies. I thought Frank had matured beyond them into the real world, but apparently not. That is how they were able to execute their little scheme under my nose. For some time now, I have been aware of Samuel's inability to cope with reality. I have the perfect excuse to rid myself of him; permanently."

Jen turned and looked at Sam.

"So you're not actually a spy?"

"Afraid not. To be fair, I never said I was."

"My mind is now officially blown."

Outside the circle of light, past the darkness, in what sounded like a completely different room, they heard a muffled explosion, followed by gunfire. Both Lassiters and Jen turned their attention toward the sounds as if caught up in a radio serial. After several minutes, a door opened and the room was flooded with light. Jen and Sam see that they have been held in a small room.

"Knock knock" a voice said as a man stepped into the room.

Sam and Jen were both taken aback.

"Bernie!", they exclaim simultaneously.

Bernie was indeed standing before them, with a smile on his face, and a briefcase in his hand.

"No one hurts Bernie's friends. I promised I look out, now I shootout. Tables turned, yes?"

"Yes, yes. A thousand times yes!" Sam said. "How about untying us?"

"How did you find us?" Jen asked. "And where did you get the army?"

"My head is a lot harder than people think. Back at your apartment, Lassiter's mole thought he could stop me from warning you about the attack, but I turned the tables on him and stuffed him in the trunk. I went to help you, but Sam had already killed the German agents. So, I went back downstairs and pretended to be unconscious while Lassiter's men kidnapped you. I followed you and here I am."

A man and a woman brought another man, wearing dark clothing, into the room. His hands were bound behind him, and a cloth bag covered his head.

Jen and Sam recognized the two escorts. The man had been at her audition; the guy with the card trick that was so intent on delaying Sam. The woman, had sold them coffee, before Jen made her great escape from the bathroom. Bernie continued.

"These are just a few friends, associates, people who owe me a favor. They've been keeping an eye on you, for me. I told you that I am important."

"That's great." Sam said with a touch of sarcasm, "Ropes? Untie?"

Bernie turned to face the elder Lassiter.

"Mister Lassiter, I have a present for you. Here is your mole." he said, indicating the bound man.

Bernie removed the bag and revealed Stan, Lassiter's chief of security.

"It was obvious, really." Bernie began, "While your underlings were following orders to bring in Frank, Jen and Sam, they didn't know why. Only someone who knew the importance of what we were after would have involved them."

"What we were after?" Jen said, trying to understand what was happening around her. "What happened to your accent? Who are you, really?"

"Mister Lassiter, whatever this guy has been telling you is a lie." Stan said, trying to command as much authority as any bound man could. "He's the gypsy cab driver we were looking for. I was disposing of him, per your orders!"

"And you failed." Lassiter said coldly. "Now, be quiet, the grown-ups are talking."

Bernie gave a nod to The Barista and she stuffed most of the bag into Stan's mouth.

Turning to Jen, Bernie said, "Jen, sweetheart, you might call me a modern day Moriarty. It's a lot easier to counterfeit bitcoins than paper money these days. The virus on that microchip would put me right out of business, and nothing interferes with business. Speaking of which, may I have the coin, please?"

"How did you know- never mind. I don't even want to know. Just untie me and it's yours."

"Mister Lassiter, would you mind untying your son and his girlfriend, please?"

As Lassiter reluctantly untied Sam and Jen, Bernie's people tied Stan into one of the vacant chairs.

"She's not my girlfriend." Sam said, sounding a little like an embarrassed school boy. Turning to face Jen, he added, "Jen, you can't trust this guy. Don't give him the microchip. Who knows what he'll do with it."

"Sam, will you shut up, please? I already told you, you make a great couple. You don't get where I am by misreading people."

"He's right, though." Jen said, motioning to Sam. "The chip is too dangerous to leave in one person's hands."

"The chip is too powerful to leave in one government's hands. I don't represent a government. I'm an interested private citizen. It is against my own best interest to do anything with this chip but to bury it in the deepest, darkest hole I can find and remove the temptation for people like my dear friend, Mister Lassiter."

"I knew I liked you." Sam said.

"Shut up, Sam." Jen said, needing quiet to think. "Seriously, Bernie, how can we trust you?"

"I've known what was happening from the beginning. It was no accident that I was there when you needed me. I had my men watching and protecting you while Lassiter was chasing his own tail. Unbeknownst to Stan, he was feeding me the same information he was selling to the Germans, as well as the Russians, Chinese, Japanese, and British Intelligence. You might say he was an equal opportunity rat-fink. So, what do you say we grab a drink, discuss the chip, your future wedding plans, and let Mister Lassiter vent his blood lust on his ex-right-hand man, Stan."

Jen and Sam try to protest, but Bernie just pushes them toward the exit.

"Don't argue, kids. Bernie knows best."

Sam and Jen left, Bernie turned back to Lassiter.

"Mister Lassiter, those two are under my protection. Should anything happen to them, I will do twice what you are planning to do to Stan."

"We have a truce, for now."

"Always a pleasure to deal with a man of his word."

"We have things to talk about. You'll be at your usual watering hole?"

"Of course. Have a nice day."

Bernie handed Lassiter the briefcase he was holding, presenting it with a slight bow and a smile. Lassiter accepted it and placed it on an empty chair as Bernie left. Opening the briefcase, he noticed a variety of torture implements. Turning the case just enough to allow Stan to see what it contained, he said,

"Oh, Stanley, it's time to separate the truth from the lies."

Looking as if he might pick up one of the implements, his hand instead, went into his jacket pocket and extracted his phone. He pushed a couple of buttons and then held it to his ear.

"Hello? It's me. Would you get Bess for me, please?"

Stan broke out in a cold sweat.

CHAPTER 45

In a quiet corner of a quiet bar, Bernie, Jen and Sam talked amongst themselves, as a small staff quietly went about their business.

"Can we leave now?" Jen asked, standing up to make her exit. "I've had just about the worst day of my life."

She turned to leave but found her path blocked by a woman who looked a little familiar.

"Where's a pretty girl like you off to in such a rush?" the woman asked.

It came to Jen in a flash. The woman with the dog she ran into on the way home from the diner. Seeing that the woman was not going to yield to her right of way, Jen sat back down. Bernie started talking.

"As unpleasant as recent events may have been, we have unfinished business that is best not left to later. I also have a few loose ends to tie up with Mister Lassiter when he's done, uh, disciplining his employee. He and I need to have a mutual understanding, if we hope to continue to coexist."

Bernie signaled to one of the staff members, who came to the table, and handed him a briefcase. Jen and Sam both realized, at the same moment, that she was the receptionist form the audition.

"Thank you, my dear." Bernie said, accepting the briefcase.

"You're just going to let him go?" Sam asked.

"Sam, he's a corrupt cog in a corrupt machine. Get rid of him, and he'll be replaced by another. While he is vicious and cruel, he is still your father."

"That man you brought in is being tortured right now by that corrupt cog." Jen added.

"Stan is a sadistic killer. Mervyn gives the orders, Stan plans and carries them out."

"Mervyn?!" Jen asked, barely able to believe her ears.

"Lassiter's first name. Mervyn Charles Lassiter. Not quite so terrifying now, is he?"

"That's cold, Bernie." Sam said, "Even I don't call him Mervyn. That's just cruel."

"So what's your real name, Bernie?" Jen asked.

"If you find out, feel free to use it. We digress. This briefcase contains one million dollars. It's yours, in exchange for the chip."

Jen, suddenly feeling on the spot, looked at Sam, for advice.

"Your call." was all Sam had to offer.

"It's tempting." Jen finally said, "And I can really use the money, but this is more important than money. You say you won't use the chip, but I can't accept that."

Motioning to the bar staff again, Bernie said, "Bring in the crucible."

At the next table, one staff member had set up a portable furnace, while the other erected a metal stand with a small ceramic cup that was placed over the furnace once all was complete.

"Jen, just to put your mind at ease, this is what we'll do. Once the crucible gets good and hot, you'll drop the chip into it. When you are satisfied that it is completely destroyed and unusable, you will walk out of here with a million dollars."

Jen looked at him in disbelief.

"Why would you give me the money once it's destroyed?"

"Because you have been put through the wringer, through no fault of your own, and deserve something for your trouble. And

someday, I may have need of your
services, just like I needed a
little help form my friends here.
With a million dollars in your
pocket, you are more likely to help
me when I need you."

"I won't do anything illegal."

"That's your choice. The money
is still yours. All you have to do
is drop in the chip and melt it into
an unusable piece of slag, problem
solved."

Jen pondered for a moment, and
finally gave in.

"All right." she said, leaning
forward and pulling the coin out of
her back pocket. "Here it is. Sam,
can I get the ring?"

Sam reached into his pocket and
pulled out both the ring and a coin.
The double cross became clear to him
as he was about to hand both to Jen.
She took the coin from his hand and
was about to take the ring when,
unexpectedly, the sound of hammers
cocking filled the room. Sam's hand
closed reflexively as all heads
turned to the front door of the bar.
Lassiter had just walked in.

"You're just in time." Bernie
said, addressing the newcomer. "We
were about to destroy the chip."

"You don't want to do that."

Lassiter said.

"Why is that?"

"In its current state, the virus is too powerful, uncontrollable. I wanted Frank Emerson to develop a way to limit its scope, focus it."

"His death put an end to that."

"No, his death delayed development. I have others working on the technology to control it. We are very close to success. With your help, you and I can have the ultimate power. Attack our enemies. You can expunge all records of your existence. You and I will be the only protected people on the planet."

"I see." Bernie said, after a moments contemplation. Turning to Jen, he continued, "Give him the chip."

At this, Sam was on his feet.

"Give it to me, Jen."

Perplexed by the turn of events, she only had one question.

"Why?"

"Because I'm his son. In spite of what he told you, Lassie won't let anyone hurt me. Not really."

Too tired to fight anymore, she reluctantly gave him the coin.

"What are you going to do?" she asked.

"I'm going to release the

virus." Sam said, pulling out his gun and pointing it at Bernie. The sound of multiple hammers cocking was again heard.

"You can't do that, people will die!" Jen protested.

Bernie motioned for the staff to lower their weapons, while keeping a constant eye on Sam. Even Lassiter had taken an interest in his son's newly discovered ruthlessness. Sam's eyes darted constantly between the three.

"A few." Sam said, addressing Jen's comment. "But once the virus is loose, my father's empire will crumble. Sorry, dad. Bernie, it's all over for you, too. Your time has passed."

"What about the rest of the world?" Jen pleaded, "The end of modern civilization?"

Sam turned his attention, and his gun, toward Jen.

"They'll adapt or they won't. I know how you feel and I respect that, I really do, but this has to be done. You want to know why I was kicked out of the agency?"

"You were not kicked out. You failed their psych evaluation." said the elder Lassiter. Then, addressing the room, "He hears voices."

"Shut up, dad!" Sam yelled, turning his gun toward his father.

(Proceed with debriefing.)

"That team you mentioned? They already developed a controller for the virus."

Sam pulled an SD chip reader from his jacket pocket and set it on the table.

"I found them shacked up together in a hotel room, celebrating. After I got my hands on this, I eliminated them. I guess with all the confusion today, you overlooked them. Now, all I need is the Wildfire chip."

(You are a go to proceed. Obtain merchandise and eliminate witnesses.)

Sam handed Jen the coin and metal ring.

"Open it."

Jen looked at him, eyes wide, shaking her head.

"Open it!" Sam emphasized his point with his pistol.

Jen took the coin and ring, put the two together and smacked the table. A gunshot was heard. Jen jumped in surprise, expecting to feel the pain of a gunshot, but it was Sam who looked down at his shirt, growing red. As he collapsed on the floor, Jen looked over to see Bernie holding a gun, smoke still coming from the barrel. Jen took advantage of the chaos, before resealing the fake coin. Lassiter stepped forward, looking at his son. The gun in his hand was smoking as well.

"I was wrong." Bernie said, addressing Jen. "You two don't make such a cute couple."

Lassiter looked up from Sam's body to Bernie, who sensed the next move, and they simultaneously brought their guns to bear on each other.

"You shot my son."

"So did you." Bernie replied.

Lassiter reflected a moment, "Point taken."

"I think there has been enough killing today, don't you?" Bernie said, releasing the hammer on his pistol and re-holstering. The staff lowered their weapons as well; finally Lassiter relaxed and followed suit.

"Perhaps you're right. Another time, then."

Re-aiming his gun at Jen, he

said, "I'll take that chip now."

"Yes." Bernie said, with a wink, "Give him the coin."

With a defeated look, Jen tossed the coin, and then the ring to Lassiter. He examined both objects.

"The other coin, if you please." he said, still pointing his gun.

Jen reached into her pocket and extracted the coin, then stepped over and placed it on the table next to Lassiter. She retreated to her original spot.

"We have a deal?" Lassiter asked Bernie.

"Of course."

Lassiter put his gun away and examined the coin and the metal ring to see how they fit together. Jen passed a hand over the crucible, dropping the chip into the bowl. Bernie sat back and smiled.

"How are you holding up?" Bernie asked.

"I don't know what to feel anymore." Jen said stepping over to the briefcase. "But I've got a million ways to figure it out."

Picking up the briefcase, she winked at Bernie.

"I earned it."

"Yes, yes you did."

Upon opening the coin, Lassiter found it empty. He turned to face Jen.

"There's your chip." she said, pointing to the crucible. "Have a nice day, Mervyn."

Jen turned and left. Lassiter watched her go, but did not follow. Bernie motioned for the staff to do something with Sam's body. Lassiter turned to Bernie with a scowl on his face.

"How did she know my name?"

"Beats me." Bernie replied, shoulders shrugged, palms upraised.

"Why did you let her go?"

"She's a smart girl. She got the better of both of us. She's earned the right, don't you think?"

"You always were too soft. No discipline."

"I prefer to think of it as talent development. A little time, a little experience, and with the seed money I just gave her, Jen might one day be a player in this little game of ours."

Motioning toward the bar, Bernie asked, "Drink?"

Lassiter just nodded as Bernie led the way. Lassiter sat on a stool as Bernie walked behind the bar, set up two glasses, then reached up to the top shelf for a bottle of Scotch. After pouring, he slid one of the glasses in front of Lassiter.

"Thank you."

"By the way, how's Bess working out for you?" Bernie asked as he came around the bar.

"She brought a casserole."

"She's a very thoughtful lady. Was it any good?"

"I don't know. I didn't have much of an appetite."

"And you call me soft."

They both raised their glasses and drained the contents.